The Valentine Quest

A Love at the Chocolate Shop Romance

Melissa McClone

TULE
PUBLISHING

Dedication

To Jane Porter and C.J. Carmichael
for making Love at the Chocolate Shop a reality!

Acknowledgements

Thank you to Professor Julie Cassiday, Professor Emily Johnson, Julia Riegel, PhD candidate, Air Force Colonel Mike Cannon (Ret.) and Mrs. Beth Cannon, Air Force veteran.

Chapter One

C UPID HAD GONE on a rampage in Marietta, Montana. The over-the-top, sappy Valentine's Day decorations covering Main Street store windows and street lamps made Nevada Parker nauseous. If not for skipping lunch, she might be sick to her stomach. February fourteenth was her least favorite holiday.

Gaze focused forward, she trudged through the white carpet of snow on the pavement with one destination in mind—Copper Mountain Chocolates where her sister, Dakota, worked. Nevada ignored the explosion of red and pink surrounding her.

The only way to escape the love-inspired decorations was to stay inside Dakota's house for the next two weeks until Valentine's Day was over. That would keep Nevada focused on her dissertation—what she should be working on right now—but she'd needed to go out this afternoon.

The winter storm predicted to bypass the small town, or leave only a dusting of snow, hadn't listened to the weather forecast. Flurries had turned into inches of accumulation on the ground. The inches would likely become feet. That meant Dakota needed her snow boots so she could walk home after work.

No problem. Nevada had a plan—as usual.

She would drop off the boots and hurry back to the house before the snow worsened and one of the crazy cupid-wannabe residents in town handed her a Valentine headband to wear. Someone had already given her a shiny heart sticker, and it was only the first of February. She couldn't imagine the frenzy as the fourteenth drew closer.

Why was this town so into Valentine's Day?

A castle constructed from gingerbread caught Nevada's attention. She took a closer look at the bakery's front window. Hearts and more hearts, including heart-shaped pies and cakes.

Nevada's muscles tightened, and she blew out a frustrated breath. The condensation hung on the cold air as if containing an imaginary exclamation point to highlight her current emotional state.

Keep walking.

The wind changed direction.

Snowflakes hit her glasses. She wiped the lens with her gloved finger, but that only distorted her vision more. If only she'd put on her contacts, but she'd been rushing to get to Bozeman, where she taught three mornings a week, and worn her glasses instead.

Her right foot skidded on the snow.

Oh, no.

She raised her arms to balance herself, but her foot slid out in front of her. Gravity took over.

Thud.

She landed on her butt.

Ouch.

Snow seeped through her pants.

Brrr. That was cold.

"Hey, are you okay?" a man asked.

"Yes."

Her glasses were too wet to see clearly, but he seemed to be wearing something on his head.

"Here." He reached out to her. "Let me help you up."

Nevada placed her palm in his gloved hand—that much she could see if she looked under her lenses. He pulled her upright. He must be strong because he didn't step back.

Wrong move because she found herself on her feet but up against his chest.

Her heart pounded. Or was that his?

He was taller than her. Six feet, at least.

Unfamiliar scents surrounded her. Earthy smells. Animals.

She stiffened, straightened, and then let go of his hand. "Thanks."

"Do you want me to call anyone?"

She brushed the snow from her backside, which was sore. "Thanks, but my ego is bruised more than anything else."

That made him laugh. "If you're sure."

"Positive."

"Okay, then." The man reached into his pocket, pulled out something bright, and handed her a red bandanna. "Wipe off your glasses. Wouldn't want you to fall again."

His words prickled. Her wet, blurry glasses had nothing to do with her fall. "I slipped on the snow."

"If you say so."

She might not be able to see his face, but the teasing note in his voice stung her pride. "I do."

"Then good luck with that." He walked away.

"Hey," she called after him. "Don't you want your bandanna?"

"Keep it."

Nevada wiped her glasses, and then she tucked the bandanna into her jacket pocket. Embarrassed and annoyed from the fall, she plodded across the street.

Each step hurt. Her bottom was wet from the snow.

Not many cars were out. People, either.

Surprising given the time of day, but then again, the snow was falling harder by the minute.

She stopped in front of Copper Mountain Chocolates. The window was decked out with hearts, cupids with arrows, and *Be Mine* signs.

Molded heart-shaped chocolates on sticks, covered with cellophane, and tied with red and pink ribbons were arranged like flowers in a pretty red vase. Fancy heart-shaped boxes and white doilies held pyramids of gourmet chocolates. Shoppers would be enticed—or guilt tripped—into spending a fortune on their valentine.

No boyfriend would be giving her a card or chocolate or flowers. She hadn't received anything last year or the year before that or...

Nevada turned toward the door. Something on the window caught her gaze—a flyer taped to the inside of the glass. She scanned the colorful, heart-decorated page.

"The Valentine Quest," she read aloud.

That sounded like a cutesy activity for couples to do together. Though the flyer said individuals, pairs of friends, or couples were welcome to enter.

Not her thing, but knowing that didn't stop her chest from tightening as if a pair of imaginary arms wrapped around her and squeezed. Hard.

Nevada tamped down the feelings of loneliness and inadequacy that swelled inside her. She didn't need that with the pressure of her dissertation and teaching bearing on her shoulders like cement pilings.

Ignore the red and pink hearts.

Ignore the gnawing feeling inside.

Ignore the memory of being rejected because you were too smart. A nerd. A freak.

She didn't need to be one half of a couple to define herself. Getting caught up in the sentimentality of a commercial holiday that arose from the feast day of a saint was ridiculous.

Nevada knew better.

If anything, her dissertation topic about romantic love as a bourgeois myth was proving itself to be as true in life as in nineteenth-century literature.

Tucking her emotions safely away, Nevada focused on the flyer. The multi-day event required participants to be smart—she was—willing to volunteer—she could—and to be adventurous—no with a capital N-O.

Not a trait of hers. Not one she cared to possess, either.

Reading was as adventurous as she got, and no one would call her spontaneous. She often skipped to the final chapter and read the ending of the story first because she didn't want to be disappointed after investing her time.

Uh-oh. Snowflakes were falling faster. Smaller ones than before. She'd better drop off her sister's boots, so she wouldn't be walking back to the house in a whiteout.

Nevada wiped her shoes on the mat outside the chocolate shop, brushed the snow from her shoulders, and then opened the door.

A bell jingled. The sound reverberated along her spine.

She wasn't a fish out of water in this small town but an alien from another universe. That was how she'd always been, even growing up, when they had her skip a grade so she wouldn't be bored in class. Changing schools every other year or so because of her father's new army assignments hadn't helped.

"Welcome to Copper Mountain Chocolates," her sister

said from behind the counter. Dakota didn't look up as she used silver tongs to fill a large box with chocolates.

The delicious smell—a mix of chocolate, vanilla, and other spices—made Nevada forget her troubles. No wonder Dakota enjoyed working here. Pure, sweet goodness defined the aroma.

Nevada walked to the counter. "I have your boots."

"Great." Dakota's smile brightened her pretty face. Her light brown hair was in a French braid, and her brown eyes matched the color of milk chocolate. She wore an indigo-blue shirt with long sleeves, dark jeans, and a copper-colored apron. "I should know better than to trust one of Dylan Morgan's weather forecasts."

Nevada unzipped her backpack, removed the plastic bag holding her sister's boots, and placed it on the floor next to the counter. "Is he the one on the radio? KCMC?"

"Yes. Copper Mountain Country radio." Dakota placed two more chocolates in the box and then closed the lid. "He's a nice guy, but an awful weatherman."

"Sounds like the station needs a better meteorologist."

"Yes, but in Dylan's defense, the weather can be unpredictable."

Dakota would feel that way. Her sister always saw the good in others. She grabbed a mug from a shelf and used a ladle to fill it with whatever was in the copper pot on the stovetop behind her.

Nevada pulled off her black gloves. She touched the seat

of her jeans—wet. Maybe she'd get into her pajamas when she got home. Why not? She had nowhere else to go today.

Dakota swirled whipped cream over the contents of the cup, sprinkled chocolate shavings on top, and pushed the drink toward Nevada. "Here's a hot chocolate for venturing out in the cold for me."

Her sister's sweet gesture didn't surprise Nevada. Dakota was always helping people and animals. She'd done that when she was a child, too.

Their mother, however, had pushed Dakota to study and work harder at school. That had only caused frustrations because academics hadn't come as easily to Dakota due to a learning disability. It hadn't helped that Nevada and their brother, York, were often in advanced classes. But the kindness Dakota showered on all—human and animal— surpassed any GPA or standardized test scores. Few had the same kind and caring heart she did.

"Thanks." Nevada picked up the mug. "This is just what I need to chase away the chill."

She took a sip. The warm liquid slid down her throat. Heavenly. Every kind of chocolate she'd tried at the shop was to die for, but this drink heated her from the inside.

Perfection.

"Did class go well?" Dakota asked.

"Not well, but better than last week. Stepping in for the original instructor is an adjustment for the students and for me."

"You'll do great." Dakota placed the box of chocolates into a large bag and tied the handles with a copper-colored ribbon. "How's the dissertation?"

"It's coming along."

Slowly, painfully so.

Thank goodness that she'd been required to turn in chapters the past couple of years or she would be flailing.

Nevada had come to Montana to find peace and quiet, a place where she could work on her dissertation. Dakota's house had sounded ideal—especially after Nevada had been hired to fill in for a college instructor who needed to take an emergency medical leave—but since arriving a couple of weeks ago, Nevada had found only distractions.

Three to be exact.

Dakota's foster animals wanted Nevada's constant attention. The two dogs, Chance and Frodo, and one cat, Kimba, were sweet, but the definition of needy unless they were asleep. That meant tiring them out, but Nevada didn't want to make her sister feel bad. Dakota loved her foster animals and doted on them like they were her kids.

"The three amigos wanted to play when I got home, so we did," Nevada added.

Dakota made a face. "You're spoiling them."

Barks, meows, and being bumped by muzzles and paws weren't easy to ignore. Playing fetch and holding a laser pointer so the red dot could be chased wasn't all bad. The three seemed to appreciate Nevada's efforts. "They miss you when you're gone."

Dakota only worked at the chocolate shop three days a week—Tuesdays, Wednesdays, and Thursdays. Nevada was looking forward to Friday. When she returned from teaching, she would close the bedroom door and catch up on her work.

"Crate the dogs. They're used to it when I'm gone."

"They bark and whimper."

"They'll stop," Dakota said. "At least Kimba sleeps most of the time."

But not always in the most convenient of places.

When Nevada had opened her laptop earlier, the white cat plopped herself on the keyboard.

"The three aren't used to having someone home during the day, so they are taking advantage of you. Don't let that happen," Dakota continued. "You're the one in charge, not them."

Nevada nodded, even though she felt more like the animals' servant.

Dakota sighed. "All of us miss Bryce and Rascal, so that could have something to do with their behavior, too."

Bryce Grayson was Dakota's boyfriend. He was over on the west side of the state for a design project and had taken his dog with him. Nevada hadn't known the guy long, but he seemed nice and made her sister happy. Bryce's dad, Walt, was also a great guy, who treated Dakota like a daughter and welcomed Nevada into the family when she'd arrived in town.

A marriage proposal seemed to be a given to those who knew the couple, but Dakota wasn't in any rush for that to happen. She'd said the two needed more time before taking the next step.

Nevada was relieved to see her sister being smart about this new relationship, but her sister's feelings for Bryce seemed different—deeper—than with past boyfriends, and he acted like Dakota was the center of his universe.

"When will he be back?" Nevada asked.

"This weekend, but only for two days." Disappointment colored Dakota's voice.

"Two days is better than none."

Dakota nodded, but her gaze clouded. "I'm realizing how Mom must have felt whenever Dad went away."

Their father, now retired, had been in the army for over thirty years. The family followed him wherever he was stationed, but deployments were another story. He'd left them for what seemed like forever when Nevada was young. Now she realized the separation had been hardest on their mom. Nevada still remembered counting the days until their father returned home by marking them off on a big calendar.

She sipped the cocoa. She'd never felt that kind of love for someone. Nothing close to it. Only crushes or attraction. Maybe the hint of possibility...

"Bryce promised he'd be home for Valentine's Day," Dakota said.

Nevada nearly choked on her drink. She coughed and then swallowed.

Not Dakota, too!

"You okay?" her sister asked.

"Fine. It's just…" Nevada wiped her mouth with her hand. "Everyone around here seems into Valentine's Day. I've never seen so many heart decorations in my life. They should rename the town Cupidville."

Dakota's shoulders dropped. "Please tell me you don't still hate Valentine's Day after all this time."

Some days it felt like yesterday, not Nevada's freshman year of college. Yes, she'd put what happened behind her, but she hadn't forgotten.

She couldn't.

No matter how hard she tried.

"Hate is a strong adjective, but it's still my least favorite holiday."

And for good reason.

She'd had a huge crush on a senior in one of her classes. He was gorgeous with an amazing body. If her Mr. Right existed, it was him. When he invited her to an off-campus Valentine's Day party, she'd thought all her dreams would come true.

He'd arrived at her dorm wearing a tuxedo and carrying a single red rose. He'd been so attentive and complimentary over dinner. They'd laughed and chatted. When he'd kissed her hand during dessert, violins had played in her head.

She'd thought she found true love. She'd put her first name with his last name to see how it sounded.

Later, at the dance, she'd been having so much fun. She thought that he was, too. And then came the big announcement complete with a drumroll. She'd been chosen out of all the other women there to receive the Cupid Crown. She'd felt like the belle of the ball and believed her life would change that night.

Her pride, however, had quickly turned to humiliation when she discovered that winning the Cupid Crown meant she'd been voted the worst date at the party and only cupid's arrow could make a guy want to have sex with her. Because of her win, her date—the antithesis of Mr. Right—had received a heart-shaped box full of cash that more than covered dinner and his tux rental.

None of the women there had known the entire evening had been nothing more than a set-up. A cruel joke with each guy paying a fee to enter his Valentine's date into the competition.

The mocking laughter still burned.

Wearing high heels and her party dress, Nevada had run back to her dorm during a thunderstorm at midnight. Her date hadn't cared. He was too busy counting his prize money.

No one else had followed her to make sure she was okay. The teasing about her winning the crown had continued until her brother York had shown up a few days later. He'd taken emergency leave after she'd called him crying and, between sobs, explaining what happened. Her brother had saved her in more ways than one with that visit. She'd been considering transferring to a different school.

Dakota's eyes darkened. "You shut down those guys and their ridiculous antics."

"Yes." Instead of transferring, Nevada had made putting an end to the annual Cupid Crown event her goal. During her junior year, she'd succeeded. "It had to be done."

"So why do you still dislike the holiday?"

"Valentine's Day only reinforces an outdated mode of courtship. Couples are forced to pretend they're happy by spending money and doing lovey-dovey things for each other."

With a dreamy expression on her face, Dakota sighed. "Some are happy."

Nevada could see that. Perhaps romantic love could transform into something more, something lasting. Their parents would celebrate their thirty-fourth anniversary next month. Something had kept them together all these years.

Love, friendship, companionship, or familiarity?

She wanted to believe in love for her sister's sake, but who knew why one couple stayed together and another didn't?

"Emphasis on some," Nevada said. "Mom and Dad. You and Bryce. But you're not the norm. To many people, Valentine's Day is a slap-to-the-face reminder of being single. Especially those who would rather be in a relationship than alone."

"What about you?"

"I'm happy with how things are right now. No need to make any changes." She didn't want to go over her views on relationships with her sister after their mom had been on Nevada about finding a guy to date for the past two months. Best not to set herself up for more rejection. "I've survived February fourteenth on my own. This year will be no different."

Dakota tsked. "Just wait until a hot guy catches your eye. You'll be singing the words to "My Funny Valentine" and running out to buy a sappy card before you know it."

"There's no room in my life for romance. I need to finish my dissertation, complete this teaching position, and then—"

"I was the same way until I met Bryce."

Sort of, but not really. Nevada loved her sister, but Dakota's life had been all about working at the chocolate shop and volunteering at an animal rescue on her days off until she met Bryce. Nothing wrong with that. Still, she didn't have any professional goals she was working for, not like Nevada did.

She raised her chin. "I have a plan."

Amusement filled her sister's gaze. "Plans change."

"Not mine." Nevada had known what she wanted to do since her sophomore year of college. Merging her two interests—foreign languages and literature—had given her a direction… a goal.

"When the right person comes along, plans don't seem as important." Dakota's tone was logical, but she looked more like a bubbly and smiling theme-park princess than a sales-clerk at a small shop.

Nevada didn't want to argue over this. She took another sip of her hot cocoa.

The bell on the door rang.

Relief washed over Nevada. They wouldn't have to keep talking about this.

"Welcome to Copper Mountain Chocolates," Dakota said on cue.

The door closed.

"Nothing like being greeted with a smiling face and a chocolate sample."

The male voice was as warm and rich as the chocolate Nevada was drinking… and familiar.

She glanced his way.

Her heart thudded.

Strands of blond hair stuck out randomly from his blue beanie. A stunning blue-eyed gaze sharpened and then met hers. A bright smile followed, and his lips parted. "Well, hello there."

Chapter Two

A S SHE STOOD in the chocolate shop, tingles shot from Nevada's chest to her toes. She swallowed. "Hi."

She had no idea who the man was, but he was gorgeous. Not in the classical pretty-boy sense, but his ruggedly handsome face could easily grace the pages of a magazine or the big screen. The cut of his coat accentuated wide shoulders. The rest of him tapered to denim-covered legs and cowboy boots.

Sexy.

Maybe the appeal of the cowboy in popular culture had some merit after all.

His grin widened. "Doesn't look like falling affected you."

Her lips parted. No wonder his voice sounded familiar. He'd been the one to help her up. A good thing she hadn't been able to see him or she might have fallen back on her bottom after she stood.

"No. I'm fine." She removed his bandanna from her pocket and held it out to him. "Thanks for your help."

He hesitated, but then took the red cloth.

"When did you fall?" Concern filled Dakota's voice.

"On my way here. Nothing to worry about." Nevada patted the side of her hip where she knew it wasn't sore. "I have enough padding to keep from hurting myself."

Her bottom still stung, but no one needed to know that. Especially him.

The man took a step back. "I'd say you have just the right amount."

Heat crept up her neck.

Not only sexy, but he was also charming.

She opened her mouth to speak, but her tongue felt like it had gained twenty pounds. A good thing she wasn't interested in dating or she might be tempted to give this cowboy a second look.

Okay, not really, and not only because he'd never be attracted to a woman like her. Dating was on her "Don't Do" list. But something about him made her feel gooey inside. A way she wasn't used to feeling.

Grinning, Dakota shook her head. "This is my sister, Nevada. She's in town for a few months."

His gaze traveled from her sister to Nevada. "You're both named after states?"

She nodded. "Our brother York was named after New York."

"That's an interesting way to name kids." The man, whose name she didn't know, oozed charm and sex appeal.

"Were the three of you named after the places you were born or conceived?"

"None of us were born in our respective states," Dakota answered much to Nevada's relief. "We don't know about the other part, but our brother thinks so."

Heat pooled in Nevada's cheeks. This was not the conversation she wanted to have with a handsome stranger. Especially one who made her want to fan herself and order frozen hot chocolate to cool off. "I never got your name."

"Excuse my manners," he said politely. "I'm Dustin Decker."

Nevada silently repeated his name. "Nice alliteration."

Lines creased his forehead. "Huh?"

Oh, no. Her throat closed. She shouldn't have said that.

This wasn't a university setting. Most people didn't talk about literary devices in their everyday conversations. She wanted to blame it on the class she was teaching, but this was how her brain worked and why people thought she was weird.

Bookworm. Grammar geek. English nerd. Word freak.

She'd been called them all and, truth was, each one fit.

She wasn't like everyone else. Never had been.

But she didn't want to call attention to her not fitting in any more than she had to.

Time for a change of subject. "Are you from Marietta?"

"I grew up around Miles City, Montana, which is northeast of Billings. Now I work and live at the Bar V5 Dude

Ranch just outside of town," he said. "How about you?"

"Nevada's getting her PhD at Columbia University," Dakota said before Nevada could answer.

"Columbia," Dustin repeated. "You live in New York City."

It wasn't a question. Still, Nevada hesitated.

She hadn't been in New York since June. She'd spent over five months doing research in Europe, and then enjoyed Christmas with her brother before heading west to Montana to stay with Dakota. Nevada's possessions, other than the clothes and books she had with her, were stored at a friend's parents' house in New Jersey.

"Yes." That seemed the easiest answer to give rather than a long explanation with more information than a stranger needed to know.

His gaze ran the length of her. "That explains the black you're wearing. I hadn't heard about any funerals taking place today."

Heat rushed up her neck. That was the second time he'd made her blush. Two more times than she'd blushed in the past year.

Forget cowboys being appealing. This one was annoying her.

"New Yorkers wear a lot of black." Her wardrobe consisted of many colors. At home or hanging out at the library, she dressed more casually, but she and her friends wore black when they went out.

"What are you studying?" he asked.

"Comparative Literature."

"Nevada speaks several languages," Dakota added with a proud smile.

"Wow." Dustin sounded more amused than impressed. "Here I thought I was doing good keeping up with the subtitles during the foreign films they show to guests at the dude ranch where I work."

Nevada understood. A college degree wasn't likely a prerequisite for him to do his job. Although she had no idea what a cowboy did at a ranch other than look hot while wearing a hat, boots, and jeans. She assumed horses were involved somehow. Maybe cows.

That would explain how he smelled when she'd been up against his chest.

"But whatever pays the bills, right?" he added.

She didn't know if he was talking about himself or her, but she nodded anyway. "So far, so good. I'm filling in for an instructor at the university, and getting a regular paycheck will be nice."

Teaching would give her money and more experience. She needed to finish her dissertation before applying for another position, but she was making a list of job possibilities—Comparative Literature, English, French, and German departments at colleges and universities across the country. Living near her sister or brother would be a bonus, and this temporary job might give her an in if a position opened, but she needed to be flexible. Working as a visiting teacher or an adjunct instructor would give her the additional experience she needed to land one of the hard-to-get tenure track positions.

Professor Nevada Parker.

That was the dream—the goal.

Once she had tenure, she would be set. No moving around from place to place as she had growing up. She would be able to put down roots and have a home—a place where she belonged. She couldn't wait for that to happen.

She was so close to setting the next part of her plan into action that she could taste success as clearly as her hot cocoa. All she had to do was make the most of her time in Marietta by working on her dissertation.

Dustin reached for a brochure sitting on the top of the glass display case. "Have people been signing up for the Valentine Quest?"

Dakota nodded. "We've received a few registrations, but there's more interest now that a vacation package has been donated for the grand prize."

That got Nevada's attention.

Their brother was leaving the air force in the springtime. He wasn't a pilot, but he worked with computers. What he did was classified. He'd mentioned rarely seeing daylight when he worked. York had been stationed in San Antonio for several years before being assigned to a new position at a base in Maryland. Both she and Dakota teased him about doing secret-squirrel cyber stuff, but York would never confirm nor deny anything. A trip would be the perfect way for him to celebrate his return to civilian life.

"What kind of vacation package?" she asked.

"An all-inclusive resort in Fiji," Dakota answered. "Very luxurious from what I've seen. They're redoing the entry forms to include info about the trip, but these ones still work."

Nevada straightened. A vacation with sunny skies and a sandy beach were just what York needed. He could relax before coming to Marietta where he planned to stay before he started working as a computer consultant.

Dustin whistled. "Sounds nice. Who donated the trip?"

"An anonymous donor," Dakota said. "The offer letter came from the same law firm in Bozeman that represented whoever donated to the animal rescue at Thanksgiving time."

"Same person?" he asked.

She shrugged. "Could be."

Nevada didn't care who donated the trip, but she was grateful. Her brother deserved something special like this.

Dustin scanned the tri-fold brochure. "I'd gladly take a tropical vacation on his or her dime."

"Tired of the winter weather?" Dakota asked.

"Among other things. A change of scenery would be good, and winter is the slow season at the ranch. Might have to give this some thought."

Dakota handed him a bag. "Here are the Bar V5's chocolates."

"Thanks." He looked at Dakota. "Are you entering the race?"

Dakota shook her head. "My weekends are reserved for Bryce."

"How about you?" he asked Nevada.

"I just heard about it."

He handed her his brochure before taking another one for himself.

A horn honked.

Dustin glanced out the front window where a large pickup idled. "That's Ty and Rachel. Thanks for having the chocolates ready, Dakota, and nice meeting you, Nevada."

The way her name rolled off Dustin's tongue sent another rush of tingles shooting through her. Not trusting her voice, she nodded.

His gaze lingered, and then he looked away. "Make sure you ladies don't hang around town too long. You don't want to be heading home in a whiteout, and that's exactly what this is going to turn into no matter what Dylan Morgan forecasted."

With that, Dustin left the shop with the bag of chocolates.

Nevada watched him go. He didn't walk with a swagger. He was limping. Not bad, but he favored his left leg.

"Dustin's a real looker, isn't he?" Dakota asked.

Nevada focused on her sister. "If you like Western-type guys."

"You seemed interested."

"No.

"You were staring at him."

Was she? Nevada shrugged. "I'm not used to seeing cowboys up close and personal."

"He's a good guy. He helped when the rescue flooded. The ranch where he works takes in barn cats, and he's one of the wranglers who spoils them rotten."

"He rides horses and herds cats?"

"Among other things."

Dakota seemed to know him well. Curiosity got the best of Nevada. "Why does he limp?"

"Dustin's a former rodeo champion. Injuries forced him to retire. That's why he's working at the Bar V5 Dude Ranch. Rumor has it he needs a knee replacement."

Huh? The guy didn't look like he was thirty. "He can't be that old."

Dakota's brow shot up. "Ever seen someone ride a bull?"

"In that movie starring Scott Eastwood."

"It's only eight seconds, but talk about a wild and unpredictable ride."

"Doesn't sound like my kind of thing."

"Or mine. But I enjoy watching. There's some nice eye candy to see."

"You have a boyfriend. A serious one."

"I can still look and appreciate." Dakota motioned to the brochure Nevada held. "You interested in signing up?"

"No, but…" Nevada wasn't ready to put the flyer back on the display case. "It would be nice if York could take a vacation after he leaves the air force."

"That would be great, but you'd have to win him a trip. Remodeling the house has eaten up my extra cash."

"I'm a bit strapped, too." A grant had supported Nevada's research trip to France and Germany. She'd be earning money by teaching, but not enough to cover an expensive vacation. "I'd still like to do something for him."

Dakota stirred the mixture in the copper pot on the stove top. "He doesn't expect anything."

True.

York never expected anything from his family, especially his two younger sisters, but he'd been surprising Nevada with cash and gift cards for the past nine years, ever since she set off for college at seventeen. After their parents retired and took off in a sailboat to see the world, he bought her plane tickets to spend time with him or Dakota during school breaks. And he was only a phone call away when she needed brotherly advice.

"I know," Nevada said. "But he deserves something."

Like an all-expenses paid vacation to Fiji.

But could she do the race?

Nevada scanned the flyer. The only qualification she met was being smart. A local like Dustin, who was not only familiar with the town but also more physically in shape, would have a huge advantage over her.

"Too bad a race like this is beyond me," she admitted.

"It's not. You're brilliant. You can do anything you set your mind to do."

Her sister had always cheered on Nevada, whether for her schoolwork or being a bench warmer on the soccer team. Dakota was doing the same now. That was what big sisters did.

And face it… If Nevada had any desire for adventure, she wouldn't have told Dustin she wasn't doing the Valentine Quest when he asked.

But she didn't, and she hadn't.

With a sigh, Nevada returned the brochure to the stack on the display case. She would figure out something else to do for her brother. Taking a chance on anything outside of her comfort zone—whether a race or a hot cowboy—wasn't going to happen.

THAT EVENING IN the Bar V5's men's bunkhouse, Dustin sat on the couch. A blizzard raged outside—rattling the windows with wind and snow—but he was dry and warm inside. Logs crackled in the fireplace. Beer bottles and a bag of chips were on the coffee table. A basketball game played on the television.

A typical winter night at the ranch.

"Foul," his bunkmate, Eli, sitting in a nearby recliner, yelled. "Put on your glasses, Ref."

Smiling, Dustin took a swig from his beer bottle. Not the same as drinking a pint of draft at Grey's Saloon and checking out the women there, but staying home was safer than being out in this weather.

"Come on," Eli shouted at the television set. "I could have made that shot."

Dustin grinned at his friend and coworker. "You could have made that shot wearing your boots, spurs, and hat with one hand behind your back."

"No hat. And two hands." Eli balled a napkin and tossed it at Dustin.

As he caught the incoming shot, one of the teams scored three points.

The wrangler from Florida jumped to his feet and pointed at the television. "Now that's what I'm talking about."

Dustin sipped his beer. Eli was more fun to watch than the game.

Eli sat. "You're quiet tonight."

"Not one of my teams."

"That hasn't stopped you before."

Dustin shrugged. "Been thinking about stuff."

"Time to move on?"

He knew Eli had been looking to see what other ranches were hiring. "Nah."

After Dustin was forced to retire from the rodeo, money

from a fund for injured bull riders had helped pay his medical and living expenses, but he hadn't want to ask for more so he looked for a job. He was grateful the Bar V5 foreman had taken a chance on a broken-down bull rider. Dustin had lived at the dude ranch for almost three years and saw no reason to leave. The bunkhouse was the ultimate man cave with weekly housekeeping service and meals cooked by a talented chef. If not for the health insurance and sick leave provided for full-time employees, he'd be bankrupt.

And likely homeless.

But a cowboy could only give so many sleigh rides and pass out hot cocoa to guests before he started losing it. Dustin was getting to that point. Especially now that he had so much time to sit around and catch up on stuff like the world he'd been forced to leave behind.

This coming weekend, the bull-riding series would be in California. He wanted to go back.

He missed the lifestyle.

He missed the competition.

He missed the ornery bulls.

The pain in his knee traveled to his heart. Squeezed.

Dustin rubbed the back of his neck. "Winter is getting to me."

"I can't wait for summer to arrive."

"You and me both." The sold-out summer season meant nonstop activities and riding. He was so busy then, he didn't miss rodeoing as much.

In the winter, he rode each morning to check the cattle and survey the grounds. Salt blocks needed to be delivered, water sources kept running, and repairs done on fences and outbuildings. But the rest of the chores and guest interactions were limited and, dare he say, boring. Not even chatting up the pretty ladies at Grey's made that big of a difference.

Dustin stared at his beer bottle. "It's way too slow right now."

"Not much we can do about that."

"Maybe there is."

He pulled out the Valentine Quest brochure from his pocket and glanced at the front page. Hearts and arrows outnumbered the words, but the event was in honor of Valentine's Day. What did he expect?

"I picked this up in town today."

"What is it?" Eli drank his beer.

"There's a race coming up. It's called The Valentine Quest." Dustin might have a bum knee and other injuries, but that didn't change his wanting to compete at something other than card and board games with guests after dinner. "Thinking about entering."

"Is that a good idea with your knee and all the other hardware holding you together?"

"It's not a running race, but a multiday adventure challenge like you see on a reality TV show." Ty would give Dustin the time off since not much was happening at the Bar

V5. "This one also has a community service component."

"They're doing that in the middle of winter in Montana?"

Good point. One that had nothing to do with his abilities.

He looked at the brochure. "I'm guessing most events will take place indoors. Especially the service tasks."

"That would make sense." Beer bottle in hand, Eli leaned forward. "Any other reason besides going stark, raving mad this winter for doing the race?"

To show others Dustin Decker was still a winner—a champion—albeit on a lesser scale than a national rodeo series, but he would never admit that aloud.

He couldn't.

A good thing he had a second reason.

"The grand prize is a vacation in Fiji for two. Imagine the smell of salt in the air and the hot sand between your toes. Been a long, lonely winter. A week of fun in the sun surrounded by sexy women in itty-bitty bikinis sounds perfect. Interested in going if I win?"

"Would be nice," Eli agreed. "But you can find pretty women closer than the South Pacific. You don't want to chance injuring yourself again."

Again.

The word echoed through the bunkhouse.

And burned in Dustin's gut.

His coworkers looked out for him, but some didn't think

he was physically capable of doing the same hard labor, especially during summertime.

Let Dustin take care of the guests. Go on a trail ride. Save seats at the rodeo.

We've got this.

Code words for Dustin couldn't handle the job.

Except he could.

He might move a little slower when his joints got stiff or ached, but he was still capable.

Fit.

Strong.

He worked out and didn't need coddling.

"I'm not an invalid." At least not yet. "And I'm not looking for a girlfriend. The women around here tell you one thing but want the exact opposite."

"True that." Eli picked at the label on his bottle. "Heard Daisy got engaged."

Daisy was a riding instructor from Livingston and Dustin's ex-girlfriend.

"Yeah, she texted me about it." Dustin thought he'd mentioned that. Guess he hadn't. "She didn't want me to hear the news from someone else."

"Nice of her."

"She's a nice person."

Her breaking up with him hadn't changed his opinion. He just wished Daisy would have remembered what he'd told her on their first date—that he wasn't a settle-down type of guy. Daisy had said she wasn't ready for a serious relationship herself, so he thought they were fine and hadn't mentioned it again. Things had been good for a year, and then she'd accused him of leading her on by not wanting to get married and broke up with him.

He'd moved on, but no more girlfriends. "I'm glad Daisy found someone who could give her what she wanted."

Eli shrugged. "Didn't take her long to find a new guy."

"A year or so."

"Still a little too quick to meet someone, date, and get engaged, if you ask me."

"Daisy was ready to settle down." Dustin drank the rest of his beer.

Unlike him.

His divorced parents had taught Dustin that marriage wasn't for him.

The paycheck-to-paycheck living, moving from ranch to ranch for jobs, and the time his dad spent on the rodeo circuit, had been too much for his mom. She'd taken Dustin when he was three and left for Idaho. After she met a man with a stable, well-paying job who didn't want the baggage of a stepson, she'd sent him back to his dad when he was six.

His dad had never remarried, and he'd done the best he could as a single parent. Still, Dustin never wanted to put his kid through divorce and hardships. If he got married and had a family, he would be doing the same thing his father did. A kid deserved better.

Besides, no woman wanted the kind of life he lived. The cowboy lifestyle made anything but casual relationships impossible. He'd let things with Daisy go too long, and, for that, he was sorry.

"You dodged a bullet." Eli grinned. "Or should I say a ball and chain?"

Dustin nodded, but he still couldn't forget Daisy's words about him leading her on. The hurt in her voice and in her eyes. He hadn't meant to cause her pain. He'd thought she'd understood and agreed things would never get serious between them. He didn't want to make another woman feel the way Daisy had. That meant finding women who only wanted to date casually or have a fling.

"A vacation romance is just what I need," he said.

No strings. No misunderstandings. No hurt feelings.

He scanned more of the brochure to make sure he wasn't missing anything. This one must be old because the grand prize was listed as a bouquet of gift cards to various shops in town. No mention of a vacation package. "The race doesn't look difficult."

The participation waiver's small print caught Dustin's attention. The wording sounded like the typical legalese companies used to protect themselves from lawsuits.

"Sounds like fun," he added.

Eli shook his head. "More like an injury waiting to happen."

"It states not all the tasks are physical." Dustin rubbed

his leg.

He would wear a brace. That might make him feel like an old man, but he'd learned precautions were necessary. Even with a bad knee and other parts that weren't working at a hundred percent, he had a feeling this race was his to win.

Eli's gaze narrowed. "You're serious about doing this?"

"Yeah, I am." Maybe winning something, even a silly Valentine event, would make him feel better.

And if he lost... well, that wasn't an option. He'd felt like a loser for way too long.

Chapter Three

THE NEXT MORNING, the weather had improved enough for Dustin to drive into town. He had errands to run for himself and for his foreman, Ty Murphy. Walls of snow lined each side of the road thanks to the snowplows, but only flurries hit the windshield.

Heat blasted from the vents on the dashboard. Music played from the radio. He tapped his thumb to the beat of a song about drinking whiskey and playing guitars. Maybe tonight he and Eli could hit Grey's. Ty still had an apartment in town in case they drank too much and couldn't drive. All the wranglers had bunked there on many occasions.

Dustin turned onto Main Street, parked, and climbed out of his truck. His feet sank into the slush on the road. Cold air stung his face and lungs, but only a few snowflakes fell from the sky. A big change from last night.

Scrape, scrape, scrape.

He looked to his left where the sound was coming from.

Wade Burns shoveled snow off the sidewalk in front of

the flower shop. The man was bundled up in a black parka, striped hat, and heavy-duty gloves.

"Good morning," Dustin said to the handyman, who did odd jobs for businesses and residents around town. "You've been working hard."

"Making the rounds." Wade leaned against his shovel. "Got a late start due to a dead battery, but I'll be caught up shortly and hit the neighborhoods after getting a hot chocolate at Sage's place."

One of the many townspeople addicted to Copper Mountain Chocolates.

Dustin grinned. "Enjoy it."

"I will."

With a wave, Dustin crossed the street. The sidewalk in front of the Java Café was clear. Wade must have started on this side.

Dustin entered the coffee shop. Music played from overhead speakers. Warm air and the smell of freshly brewed coffee surrounded him.

A small glass case displayed pastries and muffins, but he was still full from the breakfast burrito and potatoes he'd eaten at the Bar V5 breakfast buffet.

"What can I get for you this glorious morning?" a friendly barista asked. She'd joined the staff in September and only worked a few shifts a week. He didn't know her name, but she dyed her short, spiky hair to match the season. She currently had pink and red streaks.

"An Americano, please," he said. "To go."

"Coming right up."

Dustin paid, placed a tip in the jar next to the register, and then stood away from the counter to wait for his coffee. He glanced around the cozy shop.

Quiet and empty.

A woman, the only other customer, was reading a book. A coffee mug sat on her table next to a legal pad and pen. A black jacket hung on the back of her chair. The woman was wearing a black sweater, too.

That was Dakota Parker's sister, Nevada.

He hadn't known what to make of the woman yesterday. She might be book smart, attend a prestigious Ivy League school, and speak different languages, but walking around when she couldn't see through her glasses showed a lack of common sense.

Unlike her sister.

Dakota was kind and down to earth, but she could also cut to the heart of an issue and find a solution every time. Bryce Grayson was a lucky man.

Nevada Parker wasn't like her sister. Yesterday, she'd acted so prim and proper as if she belonged in an ivory tower and not with regular human beings who didn't know a predicate from a participle. If she liked to read, he assumed she enjoyed grammar, too.

He took a closer look.

The way she tilted her head and had her lips parted as

she read told him she was a bookworm. She might be present physically, but mentally she was off somewhere else and happy to be there.

That was cool. He liked reading and always picked up a book for himself whenever he took Brooklyn, his foreman's eight-year-old stepdaughter, to the library.

Nevada's hair wasn't as light as her sister's, but the length was as long. She wore a low ponytail. No glasses today. Even so, she had that smart-girl look about her. She wore little to no makeup or jewelry, not even earrings. Low-maintenance or just didn't care? Something told him the latter.

Not his type.

But she was still pretty without trying just like her sister. Nevada, however, didn't seem as warm and welcoming. Dakota had an ever-present smile whether working at the chocolate shop, volunteering at the Whiskers and Paw Pals Animal Rescue, or walking dogs around town. The definition of friendly.

Nevada had acted wary with a hesitant smile and a gaze that didn't quite know where to look.

Must be a New York thing.

Except for her blushing.

That had been unexpected.

Today, she wore a green scarf around her neck. Guess not everything she owned was black.

Nevada lowered her book and picked up her coffee.

As her mouth touched the mug, he wondered if she ever

wore lipstick. Lipstick stains on cups were sexy. He didn't mind lipstick smeared all over his face, either.

He half-laughed.

Yes, a trip to Grey's tonight was in order if Dakota's sister was bringing these thoughts to mind.

"Dustin," the barista called.

He picked up his drink. As he turned from the counter, his gaze met Nevada's. "Good morning."

She raised her coffee mug as if she could hide behind it. "Hi."

Her voice was quiet, but with no one else in the place, he could hear her.

Walking toward her gave him a better view of her eyes—hazel. More green than brown. Maybe due to her scarf. He hadn't noticed the color yesterday. The glasses or just not paying attention.

"Having a coffee before you drive to Bozeman?" he asked.

"No classes on Tuesdays and Thursdays."

He stood next to her table. "What are you reading?"

She showed him the worn front cover. Multicolored tabs stuck out from the pages. The title wasn't written in English. "*Effi Briest.*"

Dustin had never heard of the book, but a cowboy like him wouldn't have the same reading list as a PhD candidate. He preferred genre fiction. Westerns, thrillers, and the occasional mystery novel. "What language is that?"

"German."

Dakota hadn't been kidding when she sang her younger sister's praises. "What other languages do you speak?"

"French," Nevada said without hesitation. "I know a passable amount of Italian, Spanish, and Latin, but I don't consider myself fluent."

Dustin had the feeling most other people would think so and flaunt the knowledge. He liked that she didn't. "No wonder your sister is so proud of you."

Nevada's cheeks reddened. "Thanks."

There was that charming blush again.

Maybe studying in her ivory tower had something to do with how quick her skin reddened. The reaction was unexpected and cute.

Dustin glanced at the clock on the wall. He had a little time.

Nevada Parker might not be his usual type, but he'd rather talk to a pretty woman than head out into the cold with his coffee to run errands.

"Mind if I join you?" he asked.

Nevada glanced around as if to see if he was talking to her before looking up at him. "Go ahead."

Not the warmest response, but she hadn't said no. That was good enough for him.

He pulled out the chair opposite her and sat. "Good book?"

"Very." She set her book on the table. "I've read it several times. I'm reviewing sections for my dissertation."

"What are you writing about?" he asked.

When she picked up her coffee, the wariness returned to her gaze. "You really want to know?"

"I do."

Nevada took another sip and then swallowed. "Romantic Love as Bourgeois Myth: A Comparative Analysis of *Madame Bovary* and *Effi Briest.*"

"Quite a mouthful."

The corners of her mouth lifted. "Rumor has it candidates get extra points for each word in the title. Figured every little bit helped."

Dustin smiled. "Academia humor."

"Keeps our offices from feeling like tombs or recycling bins."

She had a sense of humor after all. Maybe she wasn't quite as wary as he thought. "Anyone you know writing a dissertation on The Allure of the Cowboy as portrayed by the works of Louis L'Amour and Larry McMurtry?"

"That's a new one to me." A grin reached her eyes. "Go for it."

That made him laugh. "I'd need a bachelor degree first. I didn't go to college."

"Why not?"

She probably wouldn't understand his reason, given she'd spent most of her life in school, but she'd asked, and he would answer. "Rodeo was my focus when I was a teenager, not school. I enjoyed reading, but going to college never entered my mind back then."

"What about now?"

He shrugged. "Hadn't thought about it. I'm a little old for that."

"It's never too late. Not everyone knows what they want at seventeen or eighteen, and as people get older, situations can change due to health issues, layoffs, or finances. I've taught students of all ages."

Interesting thought, but he'd chosen a different path. The right one for him. "A degree isn't necessary for what I do."

She leaned forward. "What do you do?"

"You mean besides make the ladies swoon?"

He flashed his killer smile. That was what Zack Harris, a wrangler at the Bar V5, called it. Dustin liked using that smile with the lovely women at Grey's Saloon on Friday and Saturday nights when he didn't have to be up early the next morning to work.

Nevada's smile spread. The result was a face-brightening grin. "So the cowboy allure is real?"

"Yes, ma'am. It is indeed."

Her gaze narrowed with a serious expression. She rubbed her chin. "Or could the allure be an extension of the cowboy myth perpetuated by commercial fiction, movies, and television?"

Now she sounded like a college professor. He pictured

her standing at the front of a class. Did any of her students have crushes on her?

"You tell me." He stretched out his legs. "You're the one getting a PhD."

"My specialty is nineteenth-century European literature, so Westerns and cowboy stories are a bit outside my knowledge base."

He winked. "If you want to learn more, I can help with that."

Laughing, she angled her shoulders away from him. "I'll keep that in mind."

The alarm on his phone rang. He turned it off.

"Going somewhere?" she asked.

He had errands to finish by noon. He'd set his alarm in case he got distracted.

Like now.

"The chocolate shop opens at ten," he said.

Her nose scrunched. "Didn't you pick up an order last night?"

"Those were for the Bar V5. Housekeeping leaves a chocolate on guests' pillows each night. I don't want to buy any candy." He patted his coat pocket. "I want to drop off my entry form for the Valentine Quest."

"You're signing up?"

He nodded. "Can't win the grand prize if I don't. I'm going to be the one heading to Fiji."

She sat back in her chair. "Are you that confident or just

being cocky?"

Nevada didn't sound impressed.

"Perhaps a little of both."

"At least you're honest."

"It's the truth." He remembered handing her a brochure yesterday. "Did you enter?"

"No, but…" She studied him more like a scientist than an English teacher. The only thing missing were glasses or lab goggles. "You might want to dial back calling yourself the winner before the quest has started. You don't know your competition yet. Others might want to win the grand prize as badly as you."

"Maybe, but I'm more determined."

Her gaze remained on him. She tapped a finger against her chin. "You have it all figured out."

"Pretty much." Time to go. He picked up his coffee. "It's been nice chatting, but I should let you get back to your book. I'll be on my way to the chocolate shop."

"Make sure Dakota gives you a sample. She mentioned something about salted caramels this morning."

He loved chocolate, but the salt and caramel added to the taste. "One of my favorites."

"Mine, too. The combination of flavors works well together."

That was just what he'd been thinking.

His gaze lowered to Nevada's mouth. Her lower lip was fuller than her upper one. Would her kiss be as sweet as the chocolates?

Surprisingly, Dustin wanted to find out.

"Good luck," she said.

Huh?

His gaze snapped to hers.

Had she guessed his thoughts about wanting to kiss her?

He must be slipping if she could read him so easily. "With?"

"The quest. Though it sounds like you don't need any luck. You act like it's in the bag."

Oh, right. He'd forgotten about the race.

"I do, but thanks." Dustin pushed back in the chair and stood. Truth was, he didn't want to leave, but he had to be back at the Bar V5 for a sleigh ride this afternoon. "Luck can't hurt."

"Neither can a little modesty."

He wanted to think she was joking, but her eyes looked serious. Some might be offended, but not him.

He cracked a smiled. "Yeah, but not my style. I've never been a fan of humble pie."

"Guess that leaves more for the rest of us."

Her, at least.

And that was too bad.

She seemed modest enough.

If he were book smart and spoke foreign languages like she did, he'd be sure others knew. Everyone in town for that matter.

Not Nevada Parker.

She was different from the folks he knew, especially the women, and that intrigued him.

Cowboys, rodeos, and life in Marietta were unknowns to her. He liked that she didn't know all the names, faces, and stories. Talking to her now made him want to get to know her better.

"You're in town for a few months, right?" Dustin asked.

Two little lines formed above the bridge of her nose. She stared at her book as if to say *leave me alone*.

He would but not yet.

She looked at him. If a gaze could sigh in frustration, hers just did. "Through June."

"Then I'll be seeing you around."

He flashed his most charming smile—the one that had the buckle bunnies ready to wiggle out of their sexy thongs without him saying a word. Though he had a feeling a woman like Nevada might prefer granny panties instead.

Maybe he'd get the chance to find out.

Guess he was interested in more than talking to her.

Not surprising really. Nevada only being in town a few months appealed to him. They could hang out, keep things casual, and not worry about what came next.

The only question was…

Would the smart girl from New York be interested in a fling with a Montana cowboy like him?

Probably best to wait until after the Valentine Quest was

finished to find out. He wouldn't let anyone distract him from winning the grand prize.

And that included the intriguing Nevada Parker.

AN HOUR LATER, the noise from the now-crowded coffee shop made concentrating impossible for Nevada. She placed her book into her backpack, put on her gloves, and stood. Satisfaction flowed through her. She'd finished more than she'd planned on doing. No thanks to Dustin Decker for interrupting her.

I can help with that.

She bet he could, but she didn't need *his* kind of help.

Yes, the man was gorgeous and charming, but the potent combination had played out over the centuries in disastrous ways for the women who fell for that type.

Dustin Decker was a heartbreaker. He'd flirted as effortlessly as he breathed. Despite her experience with guys like him, part of her had been flattered and attracted until…

I'm going to be the one heading to Fiji.

What kind of man discounted everyone else who might be entering the race and assumed he would win?

She put on her backpack straps.

Confidence was one thing—sexy—but arrogance was a big turn-off to her.

She walked out of the coffee shop. Something she would have done earlier if Dustin hadn't left first.

The cool air brought a shiver. No snow was falling, but

the temperature seemed to have dropped since she arrived. She double-checked her coat was zipped to the top and wrapped her scarf around the lower part of her face.

That helped.

A hot chocolate would, too.

As Nevada headed toward Copper Mountain Chocolates, red and pink splotches flashed in her peripheral vision. She kept looking forward. The chocolate shop was close enough she didn't have to let the Valentine decorations waylay her.

A man in a cowboy hat walked toward her. He was older with weathered and wrinkled skin. His jacket, jeans, and boots, however, reminded her of the clothes Dustin wore. She guessed cowboys dressed the same no matter their age.

The older man tipped his head and then made eye contact. "Good morning, miss."

The hair at the back of her neck twitched. "Uh, hi."

"Hope you have a nice day."

Looking away from him, she quickened her step and held onto the straps of her backpack.

After living in New York, overt friendliness raised a red flag. She doubted muggers roamed Main Street, especially during daylight, but for all she knew, the man could be crazy, a psychotic killer. She needed to get to the chocolate shop ASAP.

As the bell on the door jingled, she stepped inside.

Safe.

Even if the older cowboy was just being friendly.

"Welcome to Copper Mountain Chocolates," Dakota said without missing a beat from behind the counter.

Nevada shook her head. "Is the bell your signal to say those words?"

"I've been here long enough it's automatic now. Except one time when Bryce walked in."

"Love at first sight."

"Not quite." Dakota smiled. "The man could be so annoying."

That sounded like Dustin. "Could be? You mean, Bryce isn't still annoying?"

Dakota smiled. "Either he's changed or he's growing on me."

"Maybe a combination."

She nodded. "How did working at the coffee shop go?"

"Great until the shop got too crowded and noisy so here I am."

Walking to the counter, Nevada left off the part about seeing Dustin. She didn't want her sister to get any ideas that Nevada was interested in the cowboy.

"I'd like a hot chocolate and a piece of chocolate." She peered at the glass display. "What do you recommend?"

"Everything."

"A little guidance would be nice since you work here."

"Be adventurous and try a chocolate you've never had before." Dakota turned toward the pot on the stovetop and reached for a mug.

Adventurous, huh? Nevada couldn't remember the last time she'd taken a risk. Although in the grand scheme, picking a chocolate had zero consequences other than wasting her money if she didn't like it.

She stared at the artfully displayed pieces in the case and read the ingredients. Each looked delicious.

Dakota handed over a mug of hot cocoa. "Which would you like?"

Nevada shifted her weight between her feet. She was a status-quo kind of person. She liked what she liked and stuck with that. Boring, but safe. "I haven't decided."

"Close your eyes and point."

"Seriously?"

"Otherwise, you'll be standing here all day."

She frowned. "No, because I have more work to do."

"Then why are you taking so long?"

Maybe her sister had a point.

Nevada closed her eyes, touched the glass, and then opened her eyes. Her finger pointed to one type of chocolate. "I'll take a macadamia nut truffle."

"Excellent choice." Dakota rang up the sale, and Nevada paid with cash.

Using silver tongs, her sister removed a truffle from the display, placed the chocolate on a small, white plate, and handed that to Nevada. "Enjoy."

Macadamia nuts sounded exotic and tropical. That made Nevada think of Fiji and Dustin.

She pushed both thoughts out of her head, raised the truffle to her mouth, and took a small bite. The sweet and rich flavors melted in her mouth. "This is delicious."

"See what happens when you try something new?"

Nevada looked at the brochures on the display case. The Valentine Quest would be something new and completely different.

Can't win the grand prize if I don't.

Dustin might think he was going to win, but he couldn't be certain. The grand prize was up for grabs for all entrants.

One of the requirements was being smart.

She was, and that gave her an advantage.

A big one.

Well, if she entered.

She ate the rest of her chocolate, grabbed one of the brochures, and read it. "Do you think the race will be dangerous?"

"Not at all. It's about fun and community service," Dakota said. "I heard some tasks are physical, but not all of them."

Nevada's gaze zoomed in on the words *risk taking*. That wasn't a part of her vocabulary or DNA. Just look at how she'd had to pick a piece of chocolate. She couldn't make a choice with her eyes open. That didn't bode well for an adventure.

"Are you thinking about entering?" Dakota asked.

Nevada shrugged. She had no idea what she was thinking.

"Entering might be a good way for you to meet a guy," Dakota joked. "It is called the Valentine Quest."

"The only quest I'm on is to win the vacation for our brother. I don't want anything for myself, especially a valentine."

"You don't have to decide now," Dakota said. "The forms don't have to be turned in until Friday morning."

"That's tomorrow."

"Which is why you have time to think about whether you want to do this or not."

Nevada scanned the brochure. The words *adventure* and *outrageous fun* jumped out. Neither appealed to her. Truth was, they scared her.

She hated feeling out of control in a situation. But she needed to think about this logically. What was the worst thing that could happen in such a small town in February?

Not much.

That realization gave her hope.

As she read more, her doubts didn't disappear, but her desire to do something for her brother grew.

Yes, she was uncertain. No one had ever called her brave, but something told her entering the quest was the right thing to do. Not for her, but for York.

She took a breath and another. "I don't need time to think about it."

Dakota's nose scrunched. "You're going to enter?"

The disbelief in her sister's voice was clear, but Nevada wouldn't let that stop her. Neither would an image of Dustin Decker with his hands in the air as he shouted he won.

"Yes. I'm going to enter."

With a trembling hand, Nevada removed a pen from her backpack. She'd better fill out the form before she changed her mind.

Chapter Four

FRIDAY NIGHT, NEVADA stood outside Copper Mountain Chocolates. Her heartbeat roared in her ears. Not loud enough, however, to drown out the doubts that had doubled during her walk here.

Go inside.

She should. The kickoff for the Valentine Quest began in twenty minutes, and she had goose bumps from the cold. Still, her feet wouldn't budge.

What was the worst thing that could happen?

Embarrassment, injury, death.

She balled her gloved hands.

Okay, she wasn't going to die, but the first two were possibilities—distinct ones. She wanted to win the vacation for her brother, but perhaps a secondary, albeit more realistic, goal would be to finish the quest.

In one piece.

With no blood loss or broken appendages.

That would be doable. Or should be.

Perhaps York would be proud of her for trying something new, challenging, and totally beyond her capabilities, even if she didn't win the grand prize.

Her shoulders sagged as if the island of Fiji rested on her back. Maybe she should go back to Dakota's and forget the whole thing.

"Are you going inside or staying out here?" a familiar male voice asked.

Nevada's already tense muscles bunched. She didn't have to glance behind to know it was Dustin Decker. She recognized the playful tone and rich timbre of his voice. "Going in."

She forced her feet forward and opened the door. The jingle of the bell grated on her tense nerves.

He followed her. Six feet of hotness and sex appeal in a pair of boots.

"Why were you standing outside in the cold?" he asked.

She didn't dare tell him she was about to walk back to her sister's place. Someone like him would never understand. "Thinking."

That was the truth. Had she noticed the additional pink and red decorations in the shop before, she would be heading to Dakota's right now.

The place looked different. She glanced around.

The rectangle tables that held boxes of chocolate had been replaced by smaller tables surrounded by chairs. Red and pink foil-covered, heart-shaped chocolates lay on the table tops. Paper hearts hung from the ceiling.

Hearts and more hearts.

Her stomach clenched.

Don't let the decorations get to you.

"Sure looks festive," Dustin said.

"If you like this sort of thing."

"You don't?"

This was a Valentine-themed event. Hearts and lovey-dovey items were to be expected.

Still, she shrugged. "A little over the top for me."

"Too much pink and red?"

And everything else. She nodded.

A tall, middle-aged man with a warm smile greeted them. "Welcome, I'm Tim. I own the Paradise Valley Feed Store, and I am one of the quest's sponsors. You're the first contestants to arrive."

"Good," Dustin said. "I dropped off a few people at Grey's and thought I might be late."

Grey's was the saloon Dakota had mentioned. Nevada wondered if Dustin went there to meet women. A guy as good-looking as he was must not have to look hard for dates.

Must be nice.

That was, if Nevada wanted to date.

"Have a seat." Tim motioned toward the empty tables and chairs. "We'll be passing out hot chocolate soon."

"Thanks." Nevada walked to a table off to the side that would give her a good spot to observe others, removed her hat and gloves, and shoved them in a coat pocket.

"Mind if I join you?" Dustin asked.

Nevada forced herself not to shrug or say no. Chances were, she knew no one else competing. Sitting with Dustin was better than sitting alone, right? Though she had no idea why he would want to sit with her.

"Go ahead," she said finally.

He sat. Not across from her, but next to her.

Her throat tightened.

He scooted his chair closer to hers.

Nevada would have shifted to the far side of the chair, but she was afraid she might fall off. Landing on her butt in front of him once was enough, so she leaned away from him.

But nerves threatened to get the best of her.

She didn't understand why.

Yes, Dustin was attractive. On a scale of one to ten, he was off-the-chart handsome. A Western hero come to life, but she didn't know why he made her feel so insecure.

Forget being able to lecture in a large hall and receive rave reviews. Sitting here with him, she felt like a teenager again. One who couldn't think of an intelligent word to say. Very unlike her.

His knee hit her leg. "Sorry."

If he'd stayed on his side, he wouldn't have to apologize, but there was room enough at the table for her, him, and his inflated ego. Probably best if she didn't say that.

Or anything.

He unwrapped one of the heart-shaped candies. "I didn't think you were entering the quest."

His words stirred the doubts inside her. She raised her chin. "I wasn't, but I changed my mind."

"Why?"

"I kept thinking about the grand prize."

He grinned. "That makes two of us."

Except Nevada was doubting her decision to enter. If Dustin hadn't showed up when he did, she might be at her sister's house right now.

Portia Bishop, one of Dakota's coworkers, carried cups of hot chocolate on a tray. Her hair was pulled back in a ponytail, and a smile lit up the young woman's glowing face despite the dark circles under her eyes. "Would you like one?"

"Please," Nevada said.

Dustin nodded. "Me, too."

Portia set the cups on the table while somehow managing to keep the tray in front of her without a wobble or a spill from the other mugs.

This must be a special event for the chocolate shop because the young woman wasn't wearing the indigo shirt and copper-colored apron the staff normally wore. Instead, she had on a baggy, long-sleeved red T-shirt, a loosely tied pink apron covered with red hearts, black leggings, and a stylish pair of red boots. The outfit should have been over-the-top kitschy, but on her, it looked cute.

"Are you excited for the Valentine Quest to begin?" Portia asked.

Dustin picked up his cup. "Can't wait."

At least he didn't say *can't wait to win*. Progress? Or did he just want his hot cocoa?

"Should be fun." Nevada wrapped her hands around the warm mug. Emphasis on *should be*.

Her emotions bounced from anticipation to disbelief. She hadn't told her brother what she was doing, but her parents couldn't believe she'd entered. Her mom, however, thought the quest might be a good way to meet a nice man. Mom couldn't seem to understand that Nevada wasn't doing this for herself or to find a date.

This was for York.

And that was keeping her bottom in the chair. Well, her brother and Dustin. Where he sat blocked her way to the door.

"I've never done a race like this," Nevada admitted.

"Then you're in good company," Portia said. "We've never sponsored something this big, but it's time. We started doing special monthly events in October. When the Valentine Quest was suggested, we thought it would be perfect for February."

Nevada hadn't known the shop was doing events each month, but maybe she'd been too focused on the animals and the chocolate Dakota brought home instead of the actual work her sister did.

"Great event and good cause," Dustin said.

"Yes," Nevada added. "I saw the entry fees go to local

nonprofits."

Portia nodded. "Do you want me to let Dakota know you're here? She's working in the back."

"Let her work. I'll catch up with her later."

"Tell Dakota not to worry." Dustin placed his arm around the back of Nevada's chair. "I'll keep an eye on her sister."

"I'm not sure that will put her at ease." Portia half-laughed and then walked away.

Leaning forward to avoid contact with Dustin's hand or arm, Nevada sipped the hot chocolate. The perfect mixture of flavors exploded in her mouth. Just what she needed to rein in her anxiety.

"Nice music," Dustin said.

Romantic instrumental music filled the shop.

Nevada shrugged.

As Dustin studied her, his gaze narrowed. "Let me guess. You prefer Top Forty... no, classical music."

"Classical and movie soundtracks." Nevada listened to the music playing. The popular love song had been over-played for months last year. Thank goodness that she didn't have to listen to the sappy lyrics. "You'd think they'd be playing pulse-pounding, get-the-race-won tunes to set the atmosphere."

"Maybe they will once the quest begins, but this is a Valentine's event. The couples participating might be looking for a little romance."

"If a man considers a race like this romantic, he needs a lesson in romance."

Dustin laughed. "You have a point. Though this could be a fun date night."

Not by her definition. She took another sip of her hot chocolate. "*If* couples signed up."

The bell on the door kept jingling. As more people entered the shop, the noise level increased. The conversations and laughter drowned out the music.

Dustin tilted his head toward the door. "Looks like couples did."

He was motioning at the people arriving. Two by two. Smiling couples. Hand-holding couples. Old and young couples. The ages varied from early twenties to sixties.

Nevada felt like the odd woman out among the twosomes. "Lots of pairs."

"The brochure said teams of two or individuals."

"Yes…" But she and Dustin seemed to be the only solo competitors. Unless others were running late. Or just being chummy with total strangers.

She tapped her toe. That only increased her agitation level. The couples weren't the only thing bothering her. "I wasn't expecting this many contestants."

Dustin leaned back in his chair. He was the portrait of being carefree. No worry or stress on his face whatsoever when her palms were sweating.

"Everyone wants to win the vacation." His tone was casual. No hint of concern. "But I doubt everyone here will make it to the end."

Would she?

An answer didn't come immediately like she wished it had. But she had to remember she wasn't doing the Valentine Quest for herself.

For York. For York. For York.

That would be her mantra when she thought about quitting.

Nevada unwrapped one of the red, foil-covered hearts. Chocolate contained tryptophan, an amino acid used by the brain to release serotonin, which helped people relax or feel in a better mood. Maybe that would help her. She took a bite.

Dustin glanced around.

"Sizing up the competition?" she asked.

"Nice spot for doing that." His gaze sharpened with what looked like respect. "But you already knew that."

She shrugged, even though he was correct about why she'd picked this table. Although she preferred the term observing—a more pleasant word to her.

He scanned the crowd again. "These couples and pairs put individual competitors at a disadvantage."

"Having a teammate isn't against the rules."

"No," he said. "But we need to level the playing field."

"How?"

"By helping each other out."

It was her turn to stare at him. "I thought you had this won."

"Yes, but it's called hedging one's bets." The way his gaze hardened told her how serious he was. "We stand a better chance if we work together against the other pairs."

She considered his words. "You mean form an alliance like they do on those reality TV shows?"

"You watch those?" He sounded surprised.

"I have. On occasion," she clarified.

Shows like that were a guilty pleasure. One few knew about, not even Dakota or York.

"A strategic alliance is exactly what I'm talking about," he said. "We bring different strengths to the quest."

That was true. Physical versus cerebral. "There's only one prize."

"We work together until we near the finish line, and it's down to you and me. Then we're on our own."

His plan had merit. She might do better with a partner. Especially one who was physically stronger than her.

The corners of his mouth curved upward in a charming—dare she say alluring?—grin.

Her heart thudded.

Not the reaction she expected, nor wanted, to have.

"What do you say?" he asked.

No! Her gut instinct wanted her to scream that. If for no other reason than the way his smile made her feel warm all over. Except...

For York. For York. For York.

Her original goal was to win for her brother. Competing on her own would be harder, and maybe, a little of Dustin's confidence would rub off on her. She could use some.

Amusement filled his gaze. "You want to say yes."

The man was so darn cocky, but a part of her did want to say that. Which made the other part of her want to say no. *Think.*

She had to be logical about this, which was all Dustin was being, and not let emotion get the best of her.

One deep breath followed another. "Okay."

His smile spread. "Great."

She hoped she didn't regret this.

Sage Carrigan O'Dell, the owner of the chocolate shop, and three men—Tim and two who were older—stood in the front of the standing-room only crowd. More people had arrived, and the shop was jam-packed. Still, Nevada had trouble concentrating on anyone except Dustin.

Forming an alliance meant they were using each other to win the quest.

Nothing more.

All she had to do was ignore the way her gaze kept being drawn to his face. How hard could that be?

The crowd quieted.

Nevada forced her attention on the four sponsors standing in front.

"Welcome to the Valentine Quest." Sage had long, red

hair and a welcoming smile. Dakota spoke highly of working for the lovely woman. "The race will begin after this kickoff meeting and continues through this Saturday and Sunday, and next Saturday, Sunday, and Monday. The final event will be held in the afternoon on Valentine's Day, so you'll have plenty of time for romance afterward."

Competitors laughed, but not Nevada. That Tuesday would be just another day.

"On each of the seven days, you'll perform tasks that earn you points," Sage continued. "Those points will be tallied on Valentine's Day to determine who wins the grand prize—a luxury, all-inclusive vacation package to Fiji."

The participants clapped and cheered.

Nevada sipped her hot cocoa. This wasn't a summer camp activity. She wanted that vacation, but she also didn't want to embarrass herself.

"Good move not to get caught up in the rah-rah atmosphere," Dustin said in a quiet voice. "We can't allow ourselves to be distracted."

Then she'd better not stare into his blue eyes. Those distracted her, but he was correct.

Someone here—hopefully her, not him—would walk away with the prize. Everyone else would end up with nothing.

"The quest will be full of different kinds of challenges," Sage said. "The most important thing is to have fun."

"No," Dustin whispered. "The most important thing is

to win."

Nevada found herself nodding. Teaming with him would be good for her.

Anticipation over the start of the race set her nerve endings dancing.

"One more thing," Sage said. "To record your participation in the various tasks, you'll need to take selfies and post them on the Valentine Quest's page to show you finished and met the requirements."

Nevada nearly groaned. Six-year-old children could take better selfies than her.

"What's wrong?" Dustin asked.

"I'm not a fan of selfies."

"I thought women liked that kind of thing."

Nevada stiffened. She shouldn't feel offended, but she did. "Do I look like someone who would make a duck face or do a fish gape?"

"No." He studied her. "I can't imagine you doing that."

Okay, he'd agreed with her. That was good, but he'd also made her feel like an outcast. Not an unusual feeling, but not how she'd wanted to feel with the quest starting.

Was Dustin trying to psych her out?

She wouldn't put that past someone determined to win. But he couldn't consider her his competition, could he?

"Don't worry about the selfies," he added.

"Why is that?"

He reached across the table and pushed a strand of hair

behind her ear. The brush of his finger against her cheek sent a burst of tingles exploding.

And heat.

She felt like she was already on that tropical island under a blazing sun. Uh-oh.

His smile widened. "Because I'm an expert at them."

Nevada had a feeling selfies weren't his only expertise.

She swallowed. Hard.

What had she gotten herself into? And how fast could she get herself out of it?

MAKING A STRATEGIC pact with Nevada had never crossed Dustin's mind until he'd seen all the couples and pairs of competitors. Sure, he'd considered a fling, but an alliance?

He hoped he hadn't made a mistake, but what choice did he have?

Teams would hurt his chances as a solo competitor. That was something he hadn't considered. He'd also misjudged who would be entering the Valentine Quest.

Sure, there were dads with beer bellies who coached their kids' teams, moms who wore leggings, and others looking for something fun to do. He watched them as they laughed and ate chocolate as if this were a date instead of serious business. They weren't his competition.

But the others wouldn't be as easy to beat. These were the people he'd seen at the gym, running through town, or hanging out at Grey's Saloon. Quiet people who were assessing the crowd and making a game plan as he was.

Capable. Serious. Uninjured.

They were the reason he'd rethought his strategy and asked Nevada to team up. He didn't think he could win on his own. Was having a partner a brilliant idea or a huge mistake?

Time would tell.

Nevada toyed with a foil candy wrapper.

She had a gold-medal-worthy brain, but was she athletic? He hadn't thought to ask, and he couldn't tell based on her baggy clothes and padded jacket. Black. Everything she wore. Again.

If tonight's task was outside, no one would be able to see her. He would bring reflective tape tomorrow just in case. Because...

What choice did he have?

Two heads were better than one, and they didn't let just anyone into an Ivy League university and give them a PhD.

"Ready for our first task?" he asked.

She nodded. "I want to get started."

That was the right attitude. "Shouldn't be long."

The sponsors huddled together like football players. The group broke apart with a clap, and then Sage rang a bell. The ting-a-ling sound filled the shop.

All gazes returned to the sponsors. The conversations stopped. Only music could be heard. Sappy music. The kind played at the dentist.

Tension—or was that anticipation—filled the air.

"It's time for the Valentine Quest to begin!" Sage announced.

"Tonight's task is service oriented," Tim from the feed store said. His bright red sweater matched the color on his cheeks.

Nevada blew out a breath. She looked relieved, as did a few others, but Dustin saw disappointment on several faces. He memorized those people because they would be the ones to beat.

Clifford Yerks, co-owner of the Two Old Goats wine store, stepped forward. The bigger man had a wide smile and a boisterous personality. "Doing good deeds is a way to spread love around the committee. You participants are Marietta's flock of cupids."

"This is a quest, not a cotillion." Emerson Moore, a thin man with a dry sense of humor and the other co-owner of the Two Old Goats wine store, shook his head. "The participants are an army. Cupids carry bows and arrows, not rose petals."

Sage stepped forward. "Whatever you call yourself, the task will be the same. Tonight, you'll be making chocolate for residents at various retirement homes and care facilities in the surrounding areas. Four to five teams or individual contestants will be assigned to each place. Pick up an envelope on your way out so you know where to go."

"When you arrive at your location, you'll find a box with what you need to complete the task," Emerson said. "Be sure to bring the box and any remaining supplies back to the chocolate shop tonight. If you don't, you'll be penalized."

"This is not a timed event. You'll be awarded points based on your effort," Tim added. "Take selfies while doing the task, as well as when you're passing out the chocolates to the residents."

Clifford wiggled his shoulders as if excited and ready to break out into a dance. "Don't leave the shop until you hear the whistle."

Dustin rubbed his palms against his jeans. "This sounds easy."

"Have you ever made chocolate?" Nevada asked.

"No. How about you?"

"No." Her gaze darted around the shop. "I don't do much cooking unless a microwave or a panini maker are involved."

Her voice sounded hesitant. Almost timid.

That wasn't good.

"Look at all the chocolate in the display case." Hoping to calm her worries, Dustin pointed at the counter. "It can't be *that* hard to make."

Tim blew a whistle. "Go."

Chairs scraped against the floor. People bolted for the door where Portia and Dakota stood and handed out envelopes.

He stood. "And we're off."

Nevada was already on her feet. "I don't have a car."

"You can ride with me."

Portia handed Nevada an envelope and then gave him one. He handed it back.

"We're teaming up, so only need one," he said.

Two teams were in their cars and pulling away from the curb by the time he and Nevada reached his pickup truck.

"Sage said there's no time limit." Nevada stared at the fading taillights. "I don't know why they are rushing."

"Maybe they have another place to be afterward."

Or the two teams could be trying to establish themselves at the front of the pack. That was what he and Nevada should do to psych out other competitors.

He opened the passenger door of his pickup. "Hop in."

She climbed up into the seat. "I'm used to walking in town."

"That's because your sister lives close to Main Street. But when it gets so cold your teeth feel frozen, driving a couple of blocks makes sense. And you can't get a nicer ride than this Ram truck."

He closed her door, walked around the front of the truck, hopped in, and started the engine. Country music filled the cab.

"Does the little hula dancer on the dashboard add to the ride or is that just for show?"

Her lighthearted and playful tone suggested the smart

girl wasn't as serious as she appeared to be.

"A combination of both," he replied.

And a gift from a fellow competitor after Dustin had won the truck at a bull-riding event. A prize and a blessing. If he hit a rough patch or lost his job—something that had happened regularly to his dad when Dustin was growing up—he would always have this pickup to call home.

"Where to?" he asked.

Nevada opened the envelope. "Kindred Place."

"I've been there. The Bar V5 staff hosted a gingerbread-decorating night in December." He pulled away from the curb. "The place is on Bramble Lane. Close enough to walk, but not when it's so cold."

She held her gloved fingers in front of a vent. "The heat feels nice."

"Heat is good." He made a left turn.

Bet they could generate some heat of their own. An image of them fooling around on a sunny beach filled his mind. Skin against skin. Lips against lips. Sand, heat…

His fingers tightened around the steering wheel. If he wasn't careful, he would need to lower the temperature in the cab. "You said the grand prize made you change your mind."

"Yes."

"Ready for a vacation?"

"No. I want to win so I can give the trip to my older brother, York. He's leaving the air force this spring, and I thought he could use a nice vacation before starting a job in the civilian sector."

Her reason for entering impressed Dustin. "You're a lot like your sister."

"Dakota and I live totally different lives." Funny, but Nevada sounded almost offended.

"Yes, but you both think of others and put them ahead of yourselves."

She shrugged. "I guess."

Her nonchalant reaction was weird. Everyone in town loved Dakota and all she did for others, both animals and humans. "Me? I'm just in this for myself."

Nevada laughed. "At least you're honest."

Dustin nodded. The image of her with him in Fiji didn't suck. Thinking about making out with her turned him on, but that would never happen. "When I win, I'm taking my bunkmate Eli. He's a wrangler at the Bar V5, too."

Eli would be Dustin's wingman when they hit the bar at the beach each night.

He parked the truck. "Welcome to Kindred Place."

A heart-shaped flag hung on the front door of the old Victorian. A similar flag had flown outside Copper Mountain Chocolates tonight.

She leaned closer to the window. "Nice old house."

"Many in town think so." He turned off the engine. "High school kids have their prom pictures taken here. Some wedding parties do, too."

Dustin unfastened his seat belt. As he climbed out of the truck, the passenger door slammed. Guess Nevada wasn't a stickler for manners, but nothing Dustin could do if a woman didn't give him the chance to be polite.

He closed his door.

The nearest light in the parking area was out, but he could still see thanks to the others. The cool air sent a chill through him. He looked up. Smiled.

No wonder the temperature had dropped. No clouds overhead. Only millions of stars.

Nevada met him at the back of his pickup. "We should hurry."

"Look up."

"Excuse me?" she asked.

He pointed to the sky.

She glanced up. Her mouth gaped. "Oh, my, look at all those stars."

"I bet you don't see anything like that in New York City."

"The signs in Times Square are the closest thing." She slowly spun. "Wow."

"There's a falling star. Make a wish." His wish was to win the Valentine Quest. "I made one."

Her brows drew together so those two lines returned above her nose. "You wish on stars?"

"Of course."

"Wishes don't come true."

"They won't if you never make one," he countered.

"That sounds like a motivational or positive affirmation poster."

"It's the plain truth." She was like those city folks who came to the Bar V5 each summer. They wanted to have fun in the Wild West, but they couldn't push aside their preconceived notions and let loose for a week. "Think of a wish."

The slant of her mouth told him she thought this was a stupid idea. Well, he could say the same thing about her wearing so much black.

"Please," he said.

With a sigh, she closed her eyes and then opened them. "Okay, I did."

He wondered what she wished for—to win the quest or for a sexy cowboy like him to be with on Valentine's Day. The race would be over by the night of the fourteenth. Plenty of time to have a little fun together—Cupid willing.

"Come on. We're wasting time." Nevada walked toward the entrance. "Wishing isn't going to get this done."

No. Dustin followed her. But wishing wouldn't hurt.

Chapter Five

A N HOUR LATER, standing in Kindred Place's commercial kitchen, the smell of burnt chocolate brought a frown to Dustin's face. He wanted a do-over wish on the falling star.

Forget about wishing to win the grand prize. He should have wished for the skills to make heart-shaped chocolate candies.

This task sucked.

Nevada rinsed out the chocolate from the pan. "This is a mess."

"Like the spilled chocolate was earlier?"

Her brows drew together. "I apologized for that. This isn't as easy to do as it sounds."

Especially when neither of them were comfortable in the kitchen or with each other. Aligning himself with Nevada hadn't helped him at all. They'd had one mishap after another. If anything, she was holding him back.

Not that he knew what he was doing, either.

Only one other team, a married couple who hadn't

glanced his and Nevada's direction since they had arrived, remained in the kitchen. The other two teams had finished and were passing out their chocolates to residents at the retirement home.

"We're going to need to make another batch," Nevada said, as if he hadn't realized that himself.

Chances were the third batch would turn out like the first two—unusable.

He took a breath, but that didn't ease his growing frustration.

Focus on one positive thing.

A physical therapist had given him that advice after his third surgery.

Dustin tried to think of one, but his mind came up empty.

It shouldn't be that hard. Finally, he thought of something. "At least Kathy isn't here glaring at us."

"Thank goodness. She wouldn't have liked seeing the scorched chocolate."

Kindred Place's head cook, Kathy, lived in a cottage at the back of the house. She was a nice woman, but when Nevada spilled most of their first batch, Kathy's sighs had been loud enough to be heard on Main Street. Thank goodness that she'd left the kitchen before they'd overcooked the second batch.

Nevada glanced at the swinging door that led to the dining room and parlor. "The other teams are handing out their chocolates."

Was stating the obvious a habit or were nerves getting to her? Dustin wasn't the nervous type, but their efforts on this task were laughable at best. That worried him. They should be killing this one.

"Making heart-shaped candy shouldn't be this difficult." Using his phone, he searched the Internet for tips on molded chocolates. "We have to be missing a step."

Nevada held up the instruction sheet. "We've been following the directions exactly. I've checked multiple times."

"Check again." He glanced down at his red apron, which was splattered and stained. "More chocolate has gotten on us than in the molds. That can't be part of the directions."

"No—"

Cheers erupted from the man and woman on the far side of the kitchen. The two gave each other high fives, and then the man carried a pink platter out of the kitchen.

"That was their fourth batch, so we're still ahead of them," Nevada said.

Dustin grimaced. "Except they're finished, and we aren't."

Nevada peered into their box of ingredients, which had been waiting for them when they arrived. "We have enough to make two more batches."

"And if we mess up those?"

"At least we gave it our best shot. I don't want to be kicked out of the race for failing to complete a task without at least trying."

"Me, either."

The kitchen door swung open. An elderly man with hunched shoulders held hands with a much shorter woman. Both had white hair, wrinkled faces, and big smiles.

"What's going on in here?" The elderly gentleman spoke in a loud voice. "Kathy said you made a real mess, and she's right."

The woman nodded. "I hope you're going to clean up before you go. Kathy works hard enough keeping us fed."

Dustin didn't need hecklers from the sidelines watching them fail. "We will. That's part of the rules."

Nevada nodded. "But that will come after we figure out what we're doing wrong."

We was the wrong word.

He would be better off on his own. That gave him an idea.

Best to cut his losses now. They could each use the remaining ingredients to make a batch. No more teamwork or alliance. "Let's each make our own batch."

"No, no, no." The older woman stepped forward. She wasn't tall, but her green eyes were sharp, clear, and focused on him. "You have to stick together. Doing it on your own is the easy way out."

She sounded disappointed.

What did he care what a total stranger thought?

"I'm all for easy," Dustin admitted.

The woman tsked. "Your attitude explains the high divorce rate in this country. No one wants to put in the effort to make a relationship work."

That described his parents. His father had said nothing could have saved their marriage. Dustin barely remembered his mother, so he only knew what his dad had told him. This woman, however, was implying he and Nevada were a couple.

No way.

He might have considered a fling, but that wasn't going to happen during the quest and maybe not afterward. They didn't work well together. That much was clear. "We're not—"

"Winter nights are colder when you're alone," the woman interrupted. Her gaze turned serious. "Laughter and determination are the two things you need to stick together."

The man nodded. "Adele knows what she's talking about. We've been together sixty-seven years."

"That's a long time." Nevada sounded impressed.

Dustin nodded, even though he had a better chance at winning the lottery than having a lasting relationship. Commitment was a four-letter word in his vocabulary. The one thing he'd committed himself to had been bull-riding, and look how that had turned out.

But Adele didn't know that or anything about him or Nevada.

"Thanks for the advice." Dustin hoped he sounded sincere, because he meant the words. He could imagine Adele saying the same words to her grandchildren. "Much appreciated."

Nevada nodded. "You're sweet to share your wisdom, but we're just—"

"We were *just*, too, at one point. Maybe two. Or three." Adele wagged her finger. "So don't tell me you want to make your own chocolates. Working together when things get rough is the only way. Remember that. Now, tell me what went wrong with the first batch."

"First two," Nevada admitted. The pink had returned to her cheeks. "This will be our third."

The man laughed. "Or fourth given how much you both are wearing."

"Oh, Harry. Give the kids a break. They're trying." Adele shook her head. "What was your problem the first time?"

"I dropped the pot. We used what hadn't spilled, but the chocolate stuck to the molds," Nevada explained. "The second batched burned."

Harry sniffed. "That's what I smell, huh?"

Adele sighed with a what-am-I-going-to-do-with-him look that seemed to amuse her husband.

"Don't you worry." Harry's eyes twinkled. "Adele will have an answer for you shortly."

"I have one now," his wife replied. "The scorching is due to melting the chocolate too quickly. Lower the temperature and go slower."

Harry nodded once. "Melting chocolate is like foreplay."

"That's right," Adele agreed. "The longer it takes, the more success you'll have."

Nevada's cheeks went from pink to the red color of her apron.

Dustin's face burned, too. Adele and Harry were old enough to be their grandparents. Maybe their great-grandparents. Not exactly who he expected to be talking about sex. He didn't know whether to be embarrassed or jealous.

"Now for the molds." Adele tapped her fingertip against her chin. "It's been a while since I made candy. We have a kitchenette in our unit, but we like eating Kathy's meals in the dining room."

"Even so, Adele will figure out an answer." Confidence filled Harry's voice. "She always knows."

"Yes, I do." Adele straightened. "Timing is everything when you're working with chocolate. You must go slow during the melting process, but you must be quick when working with molds. If the chocolate gets stuck, put the mold in the freezer. Not for too long or you'll end up with other problems, but the cold temperature will harden the chocolate, so you can remove it."

Nevada gathered the ingredients for the next batch. "Let's try it."

Dustin liked her renewed enthusiasm, but he hesitated. What Adele said didn't sound unreasonable, but she could be wrong. Still, he didn't want to be rude to them or to Nevada.

"Okay." He would try to do this with Nevada once more. If this didn't work, he was making his own chocolates. No matter what Adele thought.

"Go slow," Adele reminded. She and Harry walked to the other side of the kitchen. "We'll stand over here, so we don't get in your way."

Forty minutes later, Dustin stared at the perfectly formed chocolate hearts. "It worked."

"Of course it worked," Adele said without missing a beat.

Harry nodded.

"The chocolates look fantastic." The happiness in Nevada's voice matched the gleam in her eyes. She looked at Adele. "Thank you for the help."

"Now it's your turn to help someone else."

Just not one of our competitors, Dustin thought to himself.

"We need to take photos," Nevada said to him.

He leaned closer to her and held out his cell phone. "One, two, three... Smile."

Dustin took the picture of the two of them with the plate of chocolates to provide evidence that they'd completed the task. "Now we can pass them out."

Nevada picked up the plate. "The first two go to Adele and Harry."

The helpful couple each took one.

"Remember... stick together," Adele said.

For now.

His alliance with Nevada hadn't been a total disaster, but suggesting they work together when he knew so little about her or what was required during the tasks had been premature.

At the first sign of trouble tomorrow, he would be ready to bail. He hoped she understood when that happened because he had a feeling they would be on their own sooner rather than later.

And a part of him hoped much sooner.

AFTER RETURNING THE box of supplies to the chocolate shop, Nevada zipped up her jacket, tugged her beanie lower over her ears, and walked outside. The temperature had dropped more, and she shivered. A good thing Dakota didn't live that far away.

"Are you walking?" Dustin asked from behind her.

She glanced back. "Yes. I'll see you tomorrow."

"It's cold and dark out. I'll drive you home."

His offer surprised her. He was angry over how badly they'd done. He hadn't said much to her since they'd left Kindred Place.

Nevada didn't want to put him out. "Are you sure?"

He nodded.

No words and she couldn't see any emotion on his face. Still, he'd confirmed the offer. She'd be stupid to say no.

"Thanks." Not only would she get home faster, but she

also wouldn't feel like a Popsicle when she walked through the door. "I appreciate it."

A minute later, she slid into the passenger seat.

Dustin closed her door.

This was the third time he'd opened the door for her. She had to give him credit for his manners. Especially when she could tell by the way his lips pressed together in a thin line that he wasn't happy with how tonight's task went.

He climbed behind the steering wheel, closed his door, and fastened his seat belt. He turned the key. The engine roared to life. After it warmed up, it brought welcome heat.

Her gloved fingers began to thaw. "One day down, six more to go."

Everything that had gone wrong at Kindred Place swirled in Dakota's mind like a whirlpool. If Dustin hadn't been there, would she have quit? She wasn't sure she wanted to know the answer.

"I hope tomorrow goes better," she said.

Dustin drove down Main Street. "It can't get any worse."

His tone showed his unhappiness with their performance tonight. He blamed her for their troubles.

"We finished," she said.

"Thanks to Adele's tips."

Lights from the dashboard cast shadows that accentuated his high cheekbones. Handsome. No denying that. But his devil-may-care attitude had disappeared when things went wrong. His frustrations and annoyance had grown quickly.

At her.

"Yes, but we completed the task and are still in the race."

"Barely," he muttered.

She had no idea what he'd expected from their alliance, but he'd been disappointed in her abilities tonight.

Maybe she was the reason they'd had so much trouble. Her brain malfunctioned around Dustin. She never knew what to say or do. That had only happened to her twice before—once when she'd been asked to tutor their high school quarterback, who she'd thought was cute, for the SATs, and again in college with the jerk who'd invited her to the Valentine Ball.

"We're not in last place," she said.

"Third from bottom."

The couple that had required four batches to make their chocolates were after them. A team that hadn't shown up were in last place.

"Do you know what happened to the team who wasn't there?" she asked.

"No idea. Isaac Litton signed up with his brother, Mark, who has Down syndrome. They're in the process of moving from Chicago, and I guess they expected to be here this weekend. I've only met them once, when they toured the Bar V5 horse barn. Seem like great guys."

"I hope nothing is wrong."

Dustin glanced her way. "You sound like Dakota again."

"Sorry for caring." Nevada's harsh tone hurt her ears, but

she didn't want to be compared to her older sister.

Dustin glanced her way. "I bet Isaac got busy or forgot. Buying a house and moving to a new state is a big adjustment. I'm sure the sponsors will make sure everything's okay. If not, I'll see what I can do."

That made Nevada feel better. "Thanks. I'd hope someone would check on me if I hadn't shown up."

"Did Dakota know you signed up for the quest?"

"Yes."

"You seem a little touchy when I mention you being like your sister," Dustin said.

This wasn't a topic Nevada wanted to discuss. "It's nothing."

"The way you keep reacting when it happens suggests otherwise."

She bit her lip.

"What's going on?" he asked.

Nevada hesitated. She barely knew the guy.

"It might help to talk about it." He reached across the cab and touched her hand. "Tell me what's going on."

Their gloves didn't allow for skin-to-skin contact, but the gesture warmed her insides. She couldn't remember the last time a man other than York had touched her.

It felt... good.

"I'm a good listener," Dustin said. "A trait developed during long, dusty trail rides with guests in the summertime."

She weighed the pros and the cons. Maybe she would feel better if she wasn't keeping this all inside. "It's my mom."

"Is she in town, too?"

"No." Nevada did not need in-person pestering. "She and my dad are sailing around the Caribbean, but she keeps calling me."

"About what?"

"Being more like Dakota."

His lips parted and then closed. "Volunteer at Whiskers and Paw Pals or some other place in town."

"I wish it were that simple." Nevada blew out a frustrated breath. "My mom wants me to go out on dates, so I can find a nice man like my sister did and settle down."

"Oh."

"Oh is right. I'm sorry. I didn't mean to take my aggravation out on you." Nevada rubbed her face. "But who would have thought having a boyfriend trumps getting an advanced degree?"

"Your reactions make sense now, but do you know why your mom is pestering you?"

"No idea. I've tried to think of a reason, but my parents' home is a sailboat. They're living their dream. I can't imagine they're ready for grandchildren yet. At least, I hope not."

"You don't want a family?"

Nevada gripped the armrest of the door. Once upon a time, she'd dreamed of having kids, an adoring husband, and a thirty-year mortgage on a house with a white picket fence, a home she would move into and stay. Forever.

No moving around every couple of years. No having her children attend multiple schools during the same grade. No limiting things they bought so they wouldn't have to be moved from place to place.

The dream of owning a house remained, but the dream of having a family had been replaced by getting tenure.

Not because she still didn't want a family, but she kept that longing buried deep because the *adoring husband* part of the dream was proving to be impossible. Men wanted to hang out or hook up with her, but no man was interested in more. She was too *nerdish* and *weird*.

"Not now. I have too much going on with writing my dissertation. Once I finish, I'll have a job search ahead of me." She kept her voice unemotional. Easy to do after years of practice. "Staying single makes the most sense."

The words came easily now that she'd said them enough.

Nevada hadn't given up without first trying. She'd asked a few friends out. No takers. The men she knew treated her with respect, and she appreciated that. None, however, showed any interest in her other than as a colleague, class-mate, or friend. She'd finally decided to save herself from rejection and focus on her studies.

A good decision. One she could live with.

Neither of her parents ever used to bother Nevada about her social life or lack of one, but Dakota's relationship with

Bryce had changed everything.

"I think my mom has finally realized how removed she and my dad are from our lives, and this is the result."

"I hope that's it, because casual dating is the only way to go."

"No significant other in your life?" Nevada asked.

"Nope, and I plan to keep it that way."

"Confirmed bachelor."

His easy grin returned—the first time since she'd spilled the first batch of chocolate. He nodded once. "Playing the field is my favorite pastime."

"I'm sure it is." An attractive man like Dustin likely had women throwing themselves at him, but that kind of carefree lifestyle wasn't flawless. "But that might get old someday."

"Doubt it." He rubbed the back of his neck. "My parents divorced when I was a kid. That soured my view on marriage."

She felt lucky her parents were still together. Several of her friends couldn't say the same thing, and some of her dad's soldiers had come home from a deployment to find their spouses had been unfaithful. Sure, there were exceptions, but the successful, long-term marriages seemed to be anomalies, not the norm.

She didn't have much personal experience in relationships, but her limited romantic encounters had left her heartbroken. Her dissertation research only reaffirmed that relationships often ended in sadness rather than happily ever after.

Art imitating life? Or perhaps art as justification? Either worked for her.

"Love isn't all hearts and violins," she said.

"Definitely not." His gaze met hers. "Looks like we share a common view on relationships."

That surprised her because they were so different. She stared at the hula girl on the dashboard. "Wish I could get my mom on board, too."

"Hey, I have an idea." His tone sounded more positive. "If your mom brings up finding a guy again, tell her the Valentine Quest demands your full attention and you must keep your distractions to a minimum. That includes dating."

Nevada looked at Dustin. "Dating would be a huge distraction."

He grinned. "Exactly."

"I will tell her that when we talk. Thanks."

"You're welcome." He stopped in front of Dakota's house. The place was dark except for the porch light. "Doesn't look like anyone's home."

Dakota must have gone over to Bryce and Walt's place. Not surprising. She was over there a lot, whether her boyfriend was in town or not. "I have a key. Thanks again for the ride home."

"I'll walk you to the door." Dustin reached for the key in the ignition.

She touched his arm. "Keep the engine running."

Her gaze met his, and something passed between them. Just a look—one she couldn't explain—but a rush of heat pooled low in her stomach.

If they were starring in a chick flick, this would be the perfect moment for one of them to kiss the other.

Except this wasn't a movie, and she would never just kiss a man. No matter how good looking he was. That just wasn't something she would do.

Even if a part of her wished she could.

She clasped her hands on her lap. "This isn't a date. I can walk myself to the door."

"I don't mind."

"I know. Please."

Dustin nodded once. "See you at nine?"

Nevada wondered what he'd say if she said no, but she wasn't ready to quit. She wasn't sure if she had something to prove to him or herself, but she wanted tomorrow to go better. If things didn't go well again, she had the feeling she would find herself on her own.

No more alliance. No more partner. No more help.

The muscles in her neck, shoulders, and back knotted into a macramé of tension.

For some reason, the thought of competing by herself terrified her more than being blamed for losing.

She raised her chin. "I'll be there."

Chapter Six

SATURDAY MORNING, DUSTIN sat inside the chocolate shop. Competitors filled the other tables. Some stood near the display shelves on the far wall. Most of the people he knew, some better than others, but he didn't feel like chatting.

Not when his and Nevada's names were second to last on the leader board. For whatever reason, Isaac and Mark Litton were no longer listed.

Dustin sipped his hot chocolate, but the thick, rich mixture didn't taste as sweet as usual.

If he didn't move up in the standings, winning the quest wasn't happening. That meant no trip to Fiji.

Losing.

He couldn't let that happen.

Taking another sip, he thought about Nevada and where she fit into this. Things had gone bad at Kindred Place last night, but he'd enjoyed talking to her on the drive to her sister's house.

Hearing Nevada's take on relationships had been... interesting. Some women went on the defensive when he talked about not wanting to settle down. Others told him he'd change his mind after he met the right woman or when he got older. As if thirty wasn't old enough to know what he wanted. Only the women who were looking for the same thing as he was reacted how Nevada had.

A sign?

This isn't a date. I can walk myself to the door.

Nevada Parker seemed like the kind of woman who would understand hanging out and having fun together. No strings fun.

Except not now.

No distractions until he crossed the finish line and won the quest.

But after that…

The bell on the door rang.

Nevada entered. Her red nose and cheeks suggested she'd walked here. Either her sister needed the car or Nevada was made of heartier stock than he thought. The temperature was in the teens with the wind-chill factor, but she was dressed for the cold.

Her hair was tucked into a green beanie that matched the scarf wrapped around her neck. The combo would be perfect for St. Patrick's Day, and it made him smile. Most of the other competitors, including himself, wore something red or pink. His was a red bandanna. Others had hats, scarves, and jackets. Nevada's glasses were red, so he didn't think she disliked the color.

Did that mean she was a nonconformist?

Or maybe too cool—too city—to dress for the occasion?

At least she wasn't wearing all black today. Her jacket and gloves were, but her jeans were blue. The faded denim hugged her hips and thighs like a second skin until the pant legs disappeared into the tops of her black snow boots. She wasn't skinny, but she looked fit.

That brought a rush of relief. Maybe today would go better than last night.

Nevada walked toward his table. She didn't look tired, but she appeared hesitant.

He downed his remaining hot chocolate, sat the cup down, and then pulled out the chair next to him. "Good morning."

She sat. "Ready for today?"

Nodding, he motioned to the leader board. "We have some serious catching up to do."

Her nose scrunched. "The other team must have dropped out."

"Yeah."

Portia arrived with a mug of hot chocolate in one hand and several pink envelopes in the other. She placed the drink and one envelope on the table. "This contains your morning task. You can open it now."

Picking up the envelope, Dustin wanted to feel a rush of anticipation, not the growing lump of dread in his gut. He looked at Nevada.

She was drinking her hot cocoa. A bit of whipped cream was on her upper lip like a little mustache.

Cute.

He stared at the envelope, but his gaze returned to the dollop of white above her lips.

Bet that would taste sweet.

He didn't mean only the whipped cream.

Whoa. Stop. No distractions.

Dustin reached over and wiped the white stuff off with his finger. "That's better."

She ran her tongue over her lips. "I should have used a napkin."

Or let him lick it off.

Wrong answer.

He forced his attention on the pink envelope. "Want to open it?"

"Go ahead." She drank more hot chocolate.

Dustin pulled out a red piece of paper covered in pink hearts and read aloud.

"Good morning. Today will be long, so be sure to re- main hydrated even though the temperature will be cold. Your first task is a physical one that you must do with another person. If you're competing solo, you'll need to find a partner for this task."

"We've got that covered." Nevada sounded pleased.

He was still waiting for more whipped cream to end up

on her face and not in her mouth.

"What else does it say?" she asked.

"You will run an obstacle course that's been set up in the park. To make things more challenging, you must piggyback your partner between obstacles."

The corners of Nevada's lips turned down. "How much do you weigh?"

He appreciated her wanting to do her share, but that wasn't going to happen. "Too much for you to carry. I've got this."

Lines formed around her mouth. Concern clouded her gaze. "Are you sure you can do this?"

Her doubtful tone annoyed him. He didn't like anyone questioning him. "Yes."

She set her cup on the table. "What about your knee?"

His muscles tensed, but he kept his expression neutral. He didn't like others finding out his weakness. "Why are you asking about my knee?"

"I heard you were injured."

Someone must have told her. Dakota? "That was a few years ago. My knee isn't a problem. I'm wearing a brace, just in case."

The tension on Nevada's face remained. Dustin swore under this breath. He didn't want her to be nervous or worry about him. That could affect her actions during the task. He didn't need that.

He touched her shoulder. "Don't worry. If my knee can

handle the summer season at the Bar V5, it can handle this."

She nodded, but she still looked uncertain.

Words weren't helping. Dustin would show her that he was fine. "Let's head over to the starting line."

Nevada took another sip of her drink and then stood. "We can see what we're up against."

They walked to the park. An arch made of red and pink balloons marked the starting and finish line. One team was on the course.

"Did we miss the official start?" Nevada asked.

"This is a timed event," he explained. "The order you go doesn't matter. They record how long it takes to complete the obstacle course and then rank the teams using that."

Her gaze narrowed. "It doesn't look too bad."

None of the obstacles seemed dangerous. Not unless someone was allergic to pink and red decorations.

He leaned close to Nevada's ear. Her hair smelled like vanilla—one of his favorite scents.

"Watch each team," he whispered. "See if there's a better way to get through the course. Note where they make mistakes and figure out what they did wrong."

Nevada shot him a sideways glance. "You're being methodical about this."

"You have to be if you want to win." The first two teams did well. "We'll need to move fast. Can you do that?"

"Yes." Her voice sounded stronger. Not quite adamant, but not hesitant, either.

Maybe they could pull this off. "I'll try not to jostle you when I'm carrying you."

"Don't worry about jostling me," she said. "I just hope I'm not too heavy."

"You won't be." *Too heavy* was a term he might use with cattle, never a pretty woman. No man in his right mind, or at least who appreciated the female gender, would use that term with one.

"Next," the obstacle course starter called. She held a clipboard.

"Hey, Rosie," he said. Rosie Linn sometimes worked at the chocolate shop. Less hours than she worked last fall, but that was before she and her brother started writing screenplays for a television series.

Rosie grinned. "First name, please."

Nevada stepped forward. "Nevada."

He followed her. "Dustin."

"You must piggyback your partner between obstacles. If you don't or if you miss an obstacle, a thirty-second penalty will be added to your total time. Any questions?"

Nevada shook her head, as did Dustin.

"Get ready," Rosie said.

Dustin stood in front of Nevada. "Hop on."

She didn't move. "I feel weird about this."

He glanced over his shoulder. "We have no choice unless you want to quit."

"It's still awkward."

"Yes, but even if we hadn't teamed up, we'd still have to find a partner."

"True."

She didn't sound convinced. He'd try again. "And it's better than if we were doing the course naked."

"We'd get frostbite."

That was where her mind went with naked?

"And hypothermia," she added.

Ivory tower. He bit back a laugh. "Hop on."

A deep inhale was followed by an extended exhale. "Ready?"

He bent his knees so she'd have an easier time. "Yes."

She hopped up. Her arms went on his shoulders. Her body pressed against his back. Her legs wrapped around him.

He held onto her thighs.

Forget being cold. His blood was simmering and would be boiling soon.

She moved, and the slight wiggle raised his temperature another ten degrees.

"Are you okay?" she asked.

"Yes." He needed to stop thinking about her body being soft in all the right places. "I've got you."

"Good, but if you need to drop me—"

"I won't."

Rosie pointed to the starting line. "3, 2, 1... Go!"

With Nevada on his back, he sprinted to the first obstacle, a tunnel with red and pink streamers hanging down from the top. She wore a heavy jacket and so did he, but her chest jiggled against his back.

Focus.

He ran into the tunnel. The streamers hit his face. More than once, he had to close his eyes.

"Aren't I supposed to get off?" she asked.

"The rules said to carry your partner between obstacles, but they said nothing about having to put you down. We were faster than the team before us." Running toward a hurdle course, he ignored a twinge in his knee. "But I can't carry you through this one."

Nevada hopped off and darted over the small hurdles.

He followed her. "You're quick."

She got on his back. "My high school soccer coach made us do jumping drills for conditioning. Guess my muscles remembered."

He hoped his muscles and body forgot what she felt like. Each time she moved, a flash of heat zigzagged through him.

Focus.

They were racing, not fooling around.

The next obstacle was rows of two tires. If football players could do this, so could he. "I'll carry you."

"Your knee."

"I'll be fine." He made it through the four rows before red-hot pain sliced through his knee. Grinding his teeth, he kept going.

And didn't drop Nevada.

But man, that hurt.

Next up was a set of hoops to run through. "You'll have to get off."

She did, and he felt some relief.

Nevada dropped down to all fours and crawled through the hoops. Her bottom wiggled.

Sexy.

Watching her, his knee didn't feel so bad now.

Oops. His turn.

Dustin crawled after her. That felt better than standing had.

By the time he reached the last hoop, she was half-jogging, half-stumbling across a cargo net that was raised several feet off the ground.

Nevada's foot slipped through. "Oh."

She landed horizontal on the netting with her leg hanging between squares.

"You okay?" he asked, ready to help her.

"Keep going." She pulled up her leg and then crawled. "I can do this myself."

He finished before her, but she wasn't too far behind him.

Next came a rope swing over a child-sized plastic pool. No way could he carry her during this obstacle, but she was already getting into position without him.

Nevada climbed up the small platform, grabbed the rope, and swung across.

Dustin clapped. "Way to go."

His turn.

His knee felt as if someone had hit him with a sledge-hammer, but he managed to cross the pool in one try and land on his good leg.

Her eyes darkened. "You're hurt."

"I'm fine." Forcing a smile—something he'd gotten skilled at doing during the long summer months—he bent slightly. "Get on."

She did.

Dustin's knee rebelled, but he kept going. Nothing was going to stop him from completing this task.

He carried Nevada across the finish line to the cheers of the spectators waiting. He recognized real estate agent Maddie Cash and Mick Meyer. Her little dog Clementine, who was the best-dressed pooch in Marietta, wasn't around. The temperature must be too cold for the Yorkie.

"You can let go of me," Nevada said.

Oh, right. Dustin was still holding her. His knee was killing him, but he liked the feel of her legs around him. "Be careful getting off."

With both feet on the ground, she bent over as if to catch her breath. Her face was flushed.

From the obstacle course, but he would like to see her look that way after kissing him.

She straightened. "We seemed to do that pretty fast."

"We did well."

Better than he expected, but his knee ached. He had enough experience to know he hadn't done any additional damage, but the extra weight he'd been carrying and the rapid movements had caused him pain.

He kept his knee bent and put his full weight on his right leg. "Bet we move up on the leader board."

"For sure." She glanced around. "We need a selfie at the finish line."

"That's right." Dustin pulled out his phone and held out his arm to get them both on the screen. "Smile."

Nevada did.

"I took a couple just in case." He checked the photos. "We're good."

Selfie-wise, yes, but his knee hurt. Badly.

What he wouldn't give for a bag of ice and ibuprofen.

"Rest your knee," she said to his relief. "I'll get the next envelope."

While she walked toward a table that had been set up with more heart-shaped balloons, he leaned against a tree. The cold from the bark seeped through his jacket, but keeping his weight off his knee was helping. He only hoped that would be enough if another physical task came next.

She returned with a pink envelope. "So far, we've got the fastest time, but over half the teams still need to go."

"Great. Let's hope our time holds up." Dustin fought the urge to touch his knee. He didn't want Nevada to know how much he hurt. "What's our next task?"

"I don't know. I haven't opened it."

Huh? He gave her a look. "Because…"

"I thought we should open it together."

That was sweet, and something her sister would do, too, but he wasn't about to say that aloud. "I opened the envelope this morning. It's your turn."

She lifted the flap, pulled out a pink sheet of paper, and read.

"Now that you've made your way around the park, it's time for another service-oriented task. Grab your lint roller—joking!—and head over to the Whiskers and Paw Pals Animal Rescue to see what you can do for the rest of the day to help the animals looking for forever homes."

"We'll be there a while, but it doesn't sound too hard," Dustin said.

"Hard?"

The excitement twinkling in her eyes made him do a double take. Nevada's skin glowed in a way he'd never seen before, and he fought the urge to reach out to her.

"We're going to win this one." Her tone was strong.

"Now you're talking." Dustin had no idea why this task was different for Nevada, but her confidence overflowed. Something he hadn't seen before. The change appealed to him.

Big time.

Now, he had to figure out a way not to let her down with his knee.

As she reread the letter, he straightened. Raw, hot pain ripped through him. He stiffened so she wouldn't notice.

Her smile widened and brightened her face.

Something inside him kicked. More like a newborn calf than a bull. Weird.

"Ready to go?" she asked.

He'd honed his acting skills the past couple of years to hide his bad days. Today would be no different. "All set."

"I can't wait to see what we have to do at the rescue. I've been there a few times with my sister. That's why I think we'll do well."

He hoped the next task required him to be in a horizontal or sitting position, but no matter how bad his knee got, carrying her through the obstacle course had been worth the pain. He liked touching her and couldn't wait for another chance to put his hands on her again.

Maybe he'd get his chance at the rescue.

TWO HOURS LATER, Nevada sat on the floor of the cat room at the Whiskers and Paw Pals Animal Rescue. A fluffy black cat named Inky lay on her lap and purred, but her gaze strayed to Dustin, who leaned his back against a nearby wall with his legs stretched out in front of him, an ice bag on his left knee, while felines of every shape, size, and color climbed on him.

Resting was good for him. He'd hurt himself from carrying her. She felt awful because she thought something like this might happen.

"It doesn't look like you're going anywhere for a while," she said.

"Nope." He scratched under a gray cat's chin. "You, either."

"This one has settled in, but that's okay." Especially being surrounded by so much purring. She'd read an article that claimed the frequency of purrs could promote healing. Maybe that would help Dustin's knee. "We're supposed to work a minimum of four hours."

"I'm comfortable. I can stay longer."

"For bonus points?"

He nodded. "And the company."

She remembered what Dakota had said about his ranch's barn cats. "You like cats."

"Yes." His gaze met Nevada's. "And you're here, too."

Her pulse kicked up a notch. Maybe two.

Not good. The awareness buzzing through her body from Dustin carrying her had finally stopped. Such a relief when her nerve endings had felt as if they were doing the cha-cha. She didn't want that nonsense to start up again.

Best to ignore what he'd said. "Well, this is my kind of task. Much better than cleaning kennels and scooping poop."

"Yeah, but they call this cat socializing," he said. "That's wrong."

"Why?"

"Cats, not humans, decide when they want to be social."

She glanced around. "That appears to be true."

Cats roamed free in this room full of cubbies, shelves with beds, and cat trees. One four-level tree was occupied by multiple cats. Some curled up in balls. Others stretched out with half of their bodies hanging off the ledges.

Nevada sighed. "Hard to believe all the animals had been adopted last Thanksgiving, and now they have this many again three months later."

"Unfortunately, there are more animals to take their place."

An orange-and-white kitty with the name *Zara* written on her collar walked up to Nevada. She scratched behind the cat's ears and was rewarded with purrs. "I can see why my sister likes volunteering here."

"Animals are the best." Dustin removed the ice pack and rubbed his knee. He leaned forward to peer out the room's glass door. "Carly and Dan Hayworth just passed by. Looks like they are taking dogs for a walk."

"Which couple are they?" Nevada asked.

"Middle-aged. He's got thinning hair and wears glasses. She's the brunette with a ponytail. Big smile and dimples."

"The one who looks like a pixie?"

"I never thought of her that way, but yes."

"I know who they are."

"They'll be one of the pairs to watch."

That surprised her. "They don't look very young."

"No, but age won't stop them," Dustin said. "They own a small ranch outside of Marietta. Working the land is better than going to the gym. They'll give their all during the quest like they do with their ranch."

She rubbed Zara while Inky slept. "Sounds like they got the right job here."

"This is more my pace today."

"How is your knee holding up?" she asked. "Be honest."

"A little sore, but that's normal." His gaze didn't dart around, nor did his voice sound any different, so maybe he was being truthful. "I've got enough pins and rods in me to set off airport metal detectors. Some movements or activities just hurt."

Nevada couldn't imagine. "I've never broken a bone."

"You're fortunate. I've lost track of the number I broke. One of the hazards of the rodeo."

She heard no regret in his voice. "Was being in the rodeo worth the injuries?"

Dustin nodded. "I'd still be riding if I could."

Her mouth dropped open. "Seriously?"

"One hundred percent." Another orange cat pawed at the blue disposable shoe covers he wore. "My dad competed in rodeos, too. It's been a part of my life for as long as I can remember."

"Where do your parents live?"

"My dad is in Colorado. Still a cowboy and working on a ranch down there. No more rodeos for him though. I'm not sure where my mom is. We lost touch a while ago."

"I'm sorry."

He shrugged, but he didn't look indifferent.

Even though her mother was a hundred percent annoying right now, Nevada couldn't imagine losing touch completely. "It's your mom's loss."

Dustin's gaze locked on hers. "That's what my dad says."

"Smart man."

"He can be. He can also be mule stubborn."

A black cat rubbed against Dustin. He picked up the feline and cuddled the cat like a baby.

Her heart bumped at the sight of him and the cat. She fought the urge to sigh. Hard to do with a rugged cowboy being so sweet and loving to a small animal.

"I grew up in ranch bunkhouses wherever my dad could find work," Dustin continued. "The rodeo was something I watched my dad do. I never understood why he loved the rodeo so much until I competed, and then I was hooked."

He'd told her that school hadn't been a priority. "What's the appeal?"

He tiled his head. "It felt like home. The rodeo was also an exciting, challenging place where no one cared if you drove an old truck or a new one—if your daddy owned his own ranch or worked on one. Your skills brought you respect; nothing else could give you that. And the pretty ladies love rodeo cowboys who wear shiny champion belt buckles."

That made her laugh. "That would be appealing."

He nodded, but his attention was focused on the black

cat.

"What's your job like now?" she asked.

"A lot of riding, caring for livestock, mending fences, and maintenance. The hours are long in the summer with all the guests, and in the fall when we move cattle, but it's a good job with benefits. Room and board are included. I've been there almost three years, and I'm not in any hurry to find another job."

"Is your boss giving you time off to do the quest?"

"I have two bosses, Ty and Nate. Both expect you to work hard, but they're also generous with time off. They thought the race would be good for me. Guess we'll find out if it is or not on February fourteenth."

"You mean when the winner is announced."

"Can't wait to hear my name called." He winked and then stared at the black cat in his arms. "I think the little guy fell asleep."

Nevada was getting a taste of that cowboy allure he'd mentioned at the coffee shop. She didn't understand the groupie mentality, but she understood the attraction.

Falling for a charming cowboy like Dustin Decker would be easy to do.

She might be tempted, but she couldn't. Wouldn't.

No more rejections and no more broken hearts had been her motto—well, refrain—for years and would continue to be so.

In New York and here in Marietta.

Chapter Seven

SATURDAY NIGHT IN Walt Grayson's kitchen, Nevada wiped her mouth with a napkin and leaned back in her chair. Four empty plates sat on the table. Not too long ago, they'd been filled with generous helpings of lasagna, green beans, and tossed salad. "Dinner was delicious, Walt, thank you."

The older man's smile spread to his eyes. "You must have worked up an appetite doing the Valentine Quest today."

"Nevada moved up to seventh place." Dakota sat across the table and held hands with Bryce. They kept sending love-filled glances at each other.

"That's fantastic." Walt clapped. "We'll celebrate with an apple pie from the Copper Mountain Gingerbread and Dessert Factory."

Bryce raised Dakota's hand and kissed the top. "That's one of my favorites. Sara Maria can bake pies like no other, though Dakota has been practicing."

Dakota beamed. "Well, you like pie so much it's the least I can do."

Bryce leaned over and kissed her on the lips. "Thank you."

Nevada no longer allowed herself the luxury of thinking about being in love, but she liked seeing her sister so happy and content. A part of her hoped to someday feel the same joy written on Dakota's face whenever she was with Bryce.

Maybe Dakota had found her Mr. Right even though Bryce had started off stubborn and self-centered. He didn't come across that way now and used the pronoun "we" more than "I."

"Just ignore the two love birds," Walt said to Nevada with a smile. "Once they start making goo-goo eyes at each other, it's best to leave them alone."

Bryce sighed. "Dad…"

"It's true," Walt said.

Dakota laughed. "Your dad is right."

Grinning, Bryce placed his arm around the back of Dakota's chair. "He usually is. Especially where you're concerned."

"Did you hear that, Walt?" Dakota asked.

Walt nodded. His blue eyes twinkled with mischief. "I wish I'd had my cell phone out to record him saying that, but at least I have witnesses."

Nevada laughed. She wouldn't put anything past the man who spoiled his sweet dog Scout and cute rat Pierre.

Having dinner with the two Grayson men reminded her of when their family got together. That hadn't happened since her parents set sail, but her mom had mentioned them coming to Marietta in May when York was here. Maybe by then, Dakota and Bryce would be engaged. That way, the focus would be on wedding planning, not finding Nevada a boyfriend.

"So, how is teaming with Dustin?" Bryce asked.

Dustin's smiling face as he held the sleeping cat popped into Nevada's mind. Her pulse picked up speed. "The first night was rough, but today went better."

She hoped tomorrow was easier on Dustin's knee and that they continued to move up in the standings.

"Just be careful." Walt reached for the pie on the counter behind him and placed it on the table. "Dustin is a nice guy, but he's a cowboy and not the settling-down type."

Unbelievable. Marietta was full of cupid-wannabes.

She'd heard from Dakota about Walt playing match-maker with her and Bryce. That seemed to have worked out well, but this was different. Better make sure everyone understood that.

Nevada kept a smile on her face. "Dustin and I are just helping each other out during the tasks. Nothing else."

Even though she couldn't forget how he'd held her on his back. His arms and hands on her thighs. That had been a turn-on. She'd been worried he'd drop her, but he hadn't even though his knee hurt.

"I'm glad to hear that." Dakota sliced the pie. "Dustin is the kind of guy who makes a great friend but a lousy boyfriend. No woman is going to tame him. Oh, she might lasso him for a time as Daisy did, but he's like the bulls he used to ride. Wild and unpredictable."

"I'm not a cowboy who rides bulls, but you could have said something similar about me back in November," Bryce said. "Cut the guy some slack."

"Let's not." The words burst from Nevada's mouth.

Three pairs of eyes focused on her. *Uh-oh.*

Dakota's gaze narrowed. "Why?"

Her sister would be the one to ask. Nevada swallowed around the massive heart-shaped lump in her throat. "I'm not interested in dating, and even if I were, can you imagine Dustin and me together?"

"No, I can't," Dakota admitted, even though Nevada had intended the question to be rhetorical. "The two of you have nothing in common."

Not exactly true, but an unfamiliar weight pressed down on Nevada's chest because, like it or not, she was attracted to Dustin. That feeling had only grown today when she saw him compete in pain during the obstacle course and give so much love to the cats at the rescue when he was hurting.

Dustin was the definition of charming, but she couldn't allow herself to fantasize. Daydreaming about the sexy cowboy would be dangerous. "We're total opposites."

A satisfied smile settled on Dakota's face. "It's a relief to hear there's nothing to worry about."

"Nothing at all." Nevada forced the words past her dry

lips. "Can I please have a slice of pie?"

STANDING OUTSIDE PARADISE Books on Sunday morning, Dustin waited for Nevada to arrive. He adjusted his thick gloves. The temperature wasn't as cold as the past two days, but his breath still hung in the air. He tested putting his full weight on his left leg.

Not bad.

The raw, knife-edged ache in his knee had turned into a dull throb. A good thing he'd skipped going to Grey's last night to stay in the bunkhouse and ice his knee. He could compete now.

But win?

That was the question. Especially with his alliance with Nevada still being a wild card.

"Good morning," she said.

He turned toward the sound of her voice and did a double-take. The ends of two braids hung out the bottom of her green hat, but she was also wearing a pink jacket. "You're not wearing black."

She held out her gloved hands. "These are black and so are my boots."

"I meant your jacket."

Nevada glanced down as if to remember what she was wearing. "Oh, the coat belongs to Dakota. She said that photos are being taken, so I shouldn't dress like I was headed to a funeral."

Good for Dakota. But, honestly, no one would think funeral given the way Nevada's jeans fit. This pair wasn't as faded as yesterday's, but the denim clung to her the same. He'd held onto those jean-clad legs. Sexy was the only way to describe them.

"The color suits you." His gaze slid from her green hat to her black boots. "You look ready for Valentine's Day."

Dustin expected a smile, but he didn't get one.

She looked at her boots. "It's just a jacket."

"It could be a lucky jacket and what we need to put ourselves into first place."

She shook her head. "Let's see what the tasks are before we start talking about first place."

"Having confidence is a good thing."

"Sometimes being the underdog is an advantage."

"Or it can lead to a blowout." He held open the door to the bookstore. "After you."

Contestants crowded into the small shop, which was owned by a sweet, gray-haired woman named Lesley who'd filled the gap left by her late husband with books. Dustin had a feeling she and Nevada would hit it off if they had time to get to know one another.

Nevada pointed to a stack of red boxes. "Bet those are for us."

"Good morning, everyone." Normally, Lesley sat on a stool behind the counter with a grin on her weathered face.

The smile was there, as were her glasses, but today she stood. "You'll find this morning's task in the red box. Grab one and find a spot. Once you complete it, you'll be told where to go next. Be sure to take selfies of yourself before, during, and after completing this task."

"You get a spot," Nevada said. "I'll grab a box."

He found a four-foot high bookcase with nothing on top.

Less than a minute later, she joined him. "It's your turn to open this one."

Dustin took a selfie of the box and then held onto it.

"Does everyone have a spot?" Lesley asked.

The crowd cheered yes.

"3, 2, 1… Go!"

He opened the box. "It's a puzzle."

"Pour the pieces out," Nevada said.

Dustin did and took a quick photo. He tried to put pieces together, but he couldn't find any that matched. "This is more complicated than I thought."

Nevada, however, put together pieces easily. "It's not so bad."

"That's due to your brilliant mind."

Her cheeks reddened. "Thanks, but all it takes is understanding spatial relations."

He liked how her emotions showed, but he wished she wasn't so modest. "That's not one of my skills. I'm relieved it's one of yours."

As she joined more pieces together, she bit her lower lip.

Dustin snapped a picture. Her ability impressed him because he doubted he'd have put together two pieces on his own.

She stuck the last piece into the puzzle. "All done."

He took a photo of the completed puzzle. That was when he noticed the words written on the three-dimensional heart.

"Come closer." He took another photo of them with the puzzle. "That should do it."

Other competitors were still piecing their puzzles together. Groans and curses filled the air. That was where he would be without Nevada.

Their alliance hadn't been a mistake.

He didn't want to give anything away to the other teams so he pointed at the words on their puzzle rather than saying them.

A mountain of fun
With the wind at your face.
And speed to zip you to the bottom.

Dakota shrugged. "No idea what that means."

He repeated the words in his mind.

Once, twice…

"I've got it." He covered the puzzle with the red box. That might deter someone from peeking. "Let's go."

As they hurried out of the bookstore, others glared at them. Validation rushed through him, except he'd had nothing to do with their success. Nevada's eye for shapes, patterns, and geometry had made the difference.

He motioned to his truck across the street. "I parked close just in case."

They hurried over and got in. He started the engine.

"Where are we supposed to go?" she asked.

"The sledding hill outside of town. The other wranglers and I take Brooklyn there." He pulled away from the curb. "That's the only place that makes sense."

"Who is Brooklyn?"

"She's the eight-year-old stepdaughter of the Bar V5's foreman, Ty Murphy, and the closest thing I'll ever have to a niece."

Or a daughter.

He pulled out of his parking spot and drove down Main Street. "Cute kid. Whip smart like you. She only wears pink and would love your jacket."

"Dakota's jacket," Nevada clarified. "I'm just glad you could decipher where to go."

"I hope I'm right."

"If not, we have a photo we can use to figure it out." She looked out the back window. "No one else is behind us. If this continues, we'll win."

Dustin laughed. He liked seeing her competitive side come out. "Now who's the cocky one?"

THE DRIVE TO the sledding hill didn't take long. Nevada didn't see anyone behind them and only one other car was in the parking lot—a compact SUV with a *Two Old Goats* wine store logo on the hatchback window.

She pressed her face closer to the window. Excitement surged. "This has to be it. There's a small table with a heart-shaped flag next to that car. Looks like we're the first ones here. Great job."

"I see it." He parked and turned off the car. "Let's make the most of our head start and hurry."

Nevada slid out of the pickup, tugged on a beanie, and adjusted her gloves. She didn't see the two older gentlemen who owned the wine shop, but three stacks of inflatable tubes sat next to the small table.

"The sleds are over here." She ran toward them. "We can each take one."

"If we do that, there won't be enough if all the teams show up at once."

She counted. He was right. "What should we do? Take turns?"

He picked up a tube. "Let's share this one."

She took a closer look and bit the inside of her mouth. "The tube looks a little small for two people."

"When was the last time you went sledding?"

"I... can't remember."

"Then come on." Carrying the tube, he hurried toward the hill. "We're wasting time."

"Right behind you." She hoped this was the correct decision, but with each step, her doubts grew, and the tube seemed to get smaller.

Two-thirds of the way up, Dustin was favoring his knee and limping.

"Want me to carry the tube?" she offered.

"It's light, and we're almost to the top."

Typical man.

Like her big brother.

York never showed weakness or admitted it. No matter what was going on in his life or where he might be, he looked out for her and Dakota. Nevada appreciated that, but she wished he understood she wanted to do the same for him.

She wanted to do the same for Dustin, too.

Nevada had surprised herself by not being totally helpless during yesterday's obstacle course. Doing that physical task had given her a needed boost, and the courage to do more.

At the top, Dustin set the tube on the snow near the edge of the sledding run and kept a hand on it. "Looks like someone was trying out the hill earlier."

"The Two Old Goats guys?"

"I wouldn't put it past Clifford and Emerson. Those boys like to have fun."

"Those boys have to be old enough to collect Social Security checks."

"True, but they're young at heart." Dustin sat in the tube

and placed his legs apart. "Get in front of me."

She gulped. The tube seemed tiny with Dustin aboard. "I don't want to hurt your knee."

"You won't. You'll be sitting between my legs."

That wasn't making her feel any more comfortable. Especially when she remembered her legs wrapped around him yesterday. Forget this being a quest. It was quickly turning into the Valentine dilemma.

Should she or shouldn't she sit?

"We can't lose our advantage." He patted the tube. "Hop on."

This was a bad idea, she had no doubt about that, but she sat between his legs anyway. She tried to keep space between her and his well, front. It wasn't easy to do on such a small tube. The hole in the middle kept her sliding back against him.

Whoever had come up with these tasks had no respect for personal space. Being carried. Now spooning while sitting. The positions were too intimate for two people who barely knew each other.

She inched forward, only to fall back again.

Her muscles bunched.

He touched her shoulder. "Relax."

That wasn't possible. "Your knee—"

"Is fine." Dustin snapped a selfie of them.

Something rustled. His jacket. He must be putting away his cell phone.

"Ready?" he asked.

No, but she knew what he'd say to that. She scooted forward. "Let's get this over with."

"It'll be fun."

He pulled her closer to him.

The space she'd wanted between them disappeared. Her bottom and back were against him.

He wrapped his arms around her. "Wouldn't want you to fly off."

Heat flowed through her veins. An ache grew inside her.

Flying off might be safer than staying seated.

A part of her liked being in his arms and so close to him.

"Here we go," he shouted.

And they were off.

Cold air hit her face.

The tube accelerated.

"Wheee!" Dustin yelled. "This is a blast."

He held her tighter. His breath was warm against the back of her neck.

Nevada's pulse raced faster than the sled. Her heart lodged in her throat. The response had nothing to do with the sledding—that part was fun—but everything to do with the man behind her.

Physical awareness buzzed through her.

Dustin was so solid, so male.

She felt safe, protected between his legs while wrapped in his arms. She missed being touched and held by a man, but as much as she liked that, she was nervous and afraid.

Nevada clutched the two handles in front of her like life-lines.

"Isn't this fun?" he asked.

Not trusting her voice, she nodded. Hopefully, he would see her head moving.

The hill flattened near the bottom. The tube slowed before coming to a stop.

She jumped off the tube as if it was about to explode. Okay, more like *she* might.

"Get back here," Dustin said. "We need another selfie."

Begrudgingly, she sat on the edge of the tube.

Dustin pulled her back against him. "Smile."

She had no idea if she was smiling, but the heat coursing through her made her feel warm and toasty. The cold temperature did nothing to cool her down.

Not good.

"We're finished," he said.

Nevada stood and looked around. "I see another flag. Clifford and Emerson must be over there."

"Let's go."

Instead of jogging, she walked. No one else had arrived yet, and she didn't want Dustin to aggravate his knee.

He kept her pace.

That told her he was hurting or he would have been going faster.

Near the flag, the two men sat in lounge chairs with champagne flutes full of what looked like mimosas. Flames danced from crackling logs in a portable fire pit positioned between them.

The larger man—Clifford if she remembered his name correctly—raised his glass. "Congratulations. You're the first to reach the pit stop."

Emerson rolled his eyes. "Puh-leze. This isn't the *Amazing Race*."

"No, it's the Valentine Quest, but I like saying pit stop."

Shaking his head, the thinner man pulled out an envelope. "Here's your next task."

Dustin took it. "Let's get to the truck."

Limping, he jogged back to the parking lot. Two more cars had arrived.

"We have to hurry." He handed her the envelope. "You can read this when we get to the truck."

"Okay, and this isn't the time for manners. Opening my own door will save us time." And he would be able to sit sooner. "Deal?"

"Deal."

A hint of respect shone in his eyes. That made her feel good, even if sledding had some challenges for her.

She climbed into the truck, buckled her seat belt, and then opened the envelope.

Dustin had the truck idling. "What does it say?"

"Flying fun you've had. Now it's time to glide. No miracle is necessary. Only blades. Will you find your heart on the other side?"

Dustin groaned.

She glanced up from the clue. His face was as white as

snow. He appeared crestfallen. "Is something wrong?"

He put the truck into reverse and backed out of the parking spot. "Our next task is ice skating across Miracle Lake."

"That sounds like fun."

"I…"

"What?"

He drove out of the parking lot. "I don't ice skate."

The confidence and bravado she'd come to expect from him had disappeared. Nevada didn't understand, but she had to push him to continue because that was what he would do for her. And had. Starting the first night.

"Ice skating isn't that hard. I learned when I was a little girl."

Dustin adjusted his hands on the steering wheel. "I know how to skate. I just don't do it anymore."

His voice was hesitant, full of uncertainty, and perhaps a touch of fear. That was so unlike the cowboy she'd competed with the past two days.

What was going on? And how could she get the real Dustin Decker back?

Because she owed him that.

If he hadn't suggested they team together, she likely would have never completed the first task on Friday night.

Who was she kidding?

If he hadn't come up to her outside Copper Mountain Chocolates, she likely would have never gone inside.

Chapter Eight

WHY ICE SKATING? Of all the winter sports, why did it have to be that?

Hands trembling, Dustin tried to calm himself by putting a death grip on the steering wheel as if his pickup could save him. Unfortunately, nothing or no one could.

He'd believed the quest was his to win, but he'd never imagined one of the tasks would involve ice skates and Miracle Lake. Unless the lake lived up to its name, he was screwed.

But he wouldn't take Nevada down with him.

He sensed her gaze on him, but he didn't dare look in her direction.

Just drive.

And he did.

Dustin appreciated her silence. She deserved an explanation, and he would give her one, but multitasking wasn't an option. He needed to concentrate on the road.

He wasn't worried about black ice, but with the hundred and one thoughts swirling through his head, his goal was to get them to their destination in one piece. Once he accomplished that, they could talk.

The sign for Miracle Lake appeared, and he turned into the parking lot. He took the first open spot, parked, and turned off the engine.

He clutched the keys. "I owe you an explanation, but I wanted to get here first."

"Talk to me as we walk." Nevada unbuckled her seat belt. "I see a table with a heart-shaped flag."

Dustin didn't want to get out of the truck. This was as close to the frozen lake as he wanted to be.

"Come on," she urged.

Swearing under his breath, he climbed out of the truck.

"So, what's going on?" she asked.

Her question was so simple, but his answer wasn't.

His insides twisted, and his breathing was shallow. He shoved his hands in his jacket pocket. His knee hurt, so he shortened his steps and fell behind. But the pain was just an excuse—if he were being honest with himself.

You're going to let her down.

Yourself, too.

As if he didn't know that.

Nevada glanced back at him, but she continued toward the table with the heart-shaped flag.

Rosie Linn stood behind the table. She must have volunteered for shifts at the various events since Portia was needed at the shop and Dakota only worked mid-week. "We meet again."

He nodded in her direction.

Rosie motioned to the table. "We have socks and skates for you to use during this task."

"Thanks." Nevada looked through the skates and picked up a pair. "What size are you?"

"Eleven, but—"

"This pair should fit you," she interrupted.

Didn't matter. He wasn't putting them on.

Rosie pointed to a bench down by the lake. "That's a good spot to put on your ice skates. You won't have far to go to reach the ice."

Nevada headed to the bench without a glance his way.

Begrudgingly, Dustin followed her. Not to put on the skates, but to tell her why he wasn't doing this task.

By the time he reached her, she was sitting and had removed one snow boot.

He sat next to her on the bench.

She pulled on an ice skate. "So…"

Dustin took a deep breath, and then he exhaled slowly. "When I was eight, I went ice skating with friends. We could have gone to a rink, but everyone wanted to go to the lake instead."

"Skating outside sounds like more fun."

He nodded. "My dad had told me not to do that because the temperatures had been too warm. I didn't listen and went. I ended up falling through the ice."

Nevada inhaled sharply. She placed her hand on his arm.

Although layers of outerwear separated them, he appreciated the gesture of comfort.

"What happened to you?" she asked.

"There must have been a current or I kicked the wrong way, but I couldn't find the opening where I'd fallen through. The water was so cold, and I was running out of air."

She gave a squeeze. "That had to be terrifying."

The memory shivered through him. He nodded.

More memories washed over him. The fear...

"I thought I was going to die. I could see my friends trying to break through the ice. I don't remember anything after that, but I ended up with hypothermia."

"How did you get out?"

"Someone had seen us out by the lake and called the police because they didn't think it was safe. A police officer saved my life." Dustin stared at the size eleven skates on the bench. "I haven't been ice skating since. Not on a lake or at a rink."

"I understand."

"My skipping this task won't affect you. We signed up to compete as individuals."

"I know, but if you don't do this, you'll never be able to catch up. You'll have no chance of winning."

He'd entered to win, but that was before. He stared at the frozen lake. "I'm good with that."

"That's eight-year-old Dustin talking. The Dustin I know will regret blowing a lead over this."

"We just met."

"I'm extrapolating based on what I've seen the past two days." She shoved the skates at him. "Put these on."

"No."

"Do you want me to do it for you?"

"No."

She laced her skate. "Get going. We don't have all day."

He hadn't expected her to act this way. "What happened to sympathy and compassion?"

"You'll get that, but not until you're wearing the skates."

"I was wrong."

"About?" she asked.

"You're nothing like your sister."

"Saying that won't make me go easier on you."

"I didn't think you had this in you."

"To be honest, neither did I." She stood.

Cursing and mumbling, he put on the skates and laced them. His fingers hadn't stopped trembling. "Satisfied?"

"Almost."

She had to be kidding. "What do you want now?"

"Come with me to the edge of the lake."

Shivers racked his body. "I can't."

"You can do this." She extended her arm. "Hold my hand. I promise I won't let go."

"Skating won't be good for my knee."

"Probably not, but this will be good for your soul."

"Huh?"

"Time to face your demons."

"You mean the lake."

"I'm speaking metaphorically."

English professors—rather, future ones—weren't like other people. "Can we metaphorically say I did when I didn't?"

"Doesn't work that way."

"I had a feeling you would say that."

"Come on." She held his hand. "Just to the edge."

Every nerve ending went on alert. "You want me on the ice."

"Yes, but getting there is the first step. The hardest one."

No kidding. He walked the short distance to the ice. Each step felt as if he'd fall through the earth even though he knew that wasn't possible.

"Now what?" he asked.

She stepped onto the ice.

Dustin stiffened. He held out his hands to be ready if she fell. Not that he could move any closer. "Be careful."

"It's solid." Nevada skated out a short distance. "I have zero tolerance for taking risks. I flip out if I see the corner of a page in a book turned down. I wouldn't do this if I wasn't sure. I'm positive it's safe because I listen to the weather forecasts each morning and know what the temperatures have been."

"Dylan Morgan doesn't make forecasts. He guesses. Some of us think he spins a wheel, rolls dice, or uses a Magic 8 Ball®."

"His forecasts aren't accurate, but the temperature readings are real." She skated to the edge and held out her hand. "Your turn."

"Go without me."

"If you get out here and don't want to continue, I will. But you have to try first."

"You keep your mean side well hidden."

"I teach freshmen who are away from home for the first time. Sometimes being nice doesn't always work, and you have to be hard-nosed."

"I had no idea your nose was as hard as a diamond." Her smile made him want to go to her. Until he remembered he was wearing ice skates. "Go."

"Not until you join me."

"You're going to be stubborn about this."

"Yes."

He would move closer if only to get her to stop acting like a fool and leave him alone. Every minute she waited for him caused her lead to dwindle.

He made his way to the edge. A dusting of snow covered the ice.

She hit the blade of her skate against the ice. "It's solid."

"So you've said." He motioned to where he was standing. "I'm here; now you go."

"Come onto the ice first."

"This is stupid."

"Maybe." A grin lit up her face. Her skates glided across the ice as if she'd done this her entire life. "Humor me."

"Fine." With an unsteady movement, he stepped onto the ice. "I did it. Now go."

Beaming with pride, Nevada grabbed both of his hands and pulled him forward.

"Stop," he yelled.

She did, but she kept hold of his hands. "Solid."

His ankles turned in. The position of his feet added pressure to his bad knee. "I want to go back."

"The other side isn't that far."

"Looks far to me." Admitting he was hurting both mentally and physically wasn't easy, but if doing so kept him on this side of the lake... "My knee—"

"I'll pull you across." She did some fancy footwork. "It's been a few years, but I remember how to skate."

"I see that."

Her gaze locked on his. "I'm not the strongest or fastest in the quest. Far from it, but I would never do anything to hurt you. Please. Trust me."

He was far enough from the edge he doubted he could get back on his own. If she was as risk-adverse as she said, and Dustin believed her to be, he should be safe enough. At least he hoped so. But he had no doubt he'd made an alliance with a devil disguised as a graduate student.

"Okay," he said finally. "But go slow."

"I will."

He held onto her hands as if his life depended on her. At this moment, it did.

Skating backward, she pulled him across the lake.

"Look at you." Excitement filled her voice. "You're ice skating."

"No, you are." Dustin focused on her pretty face. Nothing else, because if he thought too much about what was happening, he would fall. He was a terrible skater. His injuries didn't help. "But I appreciate the thought."

He also appreciated Nevada.

He'd faced the meanest, toughest bulls that could have killed him if they tried hard enough, but he'd let frozen water paralyze him. He hadn't realized how badly he needed to do this.

But Nevada had.

Her smile widened. "We're almost to the other side."

He looked over her shoulder. His mouth dropped open. "I..."

Dustin was speechless.

"Do you think you can take a selfie of us skating?" she asked. "If not, I can try."

"Stop for a minute."

She did.

With a deep breath, Dustin let go of one of her hands, reached into his pocket, and pulled out his cell phone. He held it up high so he could take two full-length shots of them. "Got it."

His phone went back into his pocket, and his hand held hers again.

Minutes later, they reached the other side.

Dustin stepped off the ice. Gratitude filled him. "Thank you for pushing me to do this. I apologize for all the name calling."

"I didn't hear anything other than hard-nosed, and I called myself that."

"The names were in my head."

She laughed. "Apology accepted."

"There's the box with our next task."

"Stay here. I'll get it." She grabbed an envelope and handed it to him. "I opened the last one."

"I skated across the lake. You do it."

She did. "The good news is the next task is a picture scavenger hunt through town."

"What's the bad news?"

"We have to skate back to the other side."

"I wouldn't have been able to cross the lake without your help," he admitted. "If you're with me on the way back, I can do it."

"Does that mean I didn't push you too hard?"

"No, you did, but that's the only thing that made me get out here, and I'm grateful for that. For you."

She held his hand. "You've got this."

With her help, Dustin did.

The return trip was easier for him, but the reason was all Nevada. Before they reached the other side, he stopped.

Concern clouded her gaze. Lines creased her forehead. "What?"

"I want to take another picture."

"For the quest?"

"No, for me."

Her genuine smile made everything seem right with the world. She leaned forward, and he met her halfway.

Dustin didn't have to tell her to smile. He hit the button on his phone. "Got it."

"Can I get a copy of that?"

"I'll send you all of them."

"Thanks."

"No, thank you." He kissed her. An impromptu act, just a peck on the lips, but he'd felt compelled. "I had no idea how badly I needed to do this, but you did. And I owe you."

Her face glowed. "You don't owe me, but if any tasks involve animal organs, weird food, reptiles, or bugs, you're doing those, okay?"

He laughed, something he never expected to be doing standing on a frozen lake with ice skates on his feet. "Perfectly okay."

He stepped off the ice.

Four people carried skates and were walking toward the bench. Even after her coaxing and his hesitation, they hadn't lost much time.

Maybe winning this race *was* meant to be. Meeting Nevada seemed to be.

"Let's get these skates off and head over to Main Street," he said.

EVEN WITHOUT THE street lamps or the miniature white lights twinkling on Main Street, Nevada felt as if she were in a theme park, not a real small town. The Valentine decorations played a big role in that, but so did the man walking on her left. A kaleidoscope of emotions flashed inside her—pride, happiness, excitement, anticipation, and attraction.

So much of the latter.

The last thing she'd ever expected was for Dustin to kiss her. Granted, the peck lasted less than a nanosecond, but he'd surprised her and she was... touched. Her lips—and her, too—wanted another kiss, if only to have time to feel it and react, not stand there dumbfounded and trying not to fall.

Dustin glanced at his cell phone. "We've got the required pictures on this street."

He was taking the lead for the photo scavenger hunt. This was his town, and after watching him conquer his fear and skate across the lake, she was ready to concede. This was his race to win, and she'd do what she could to help him. She hoped York would be happy and proud that she'd participated.

She glanced over at Dustin. "Just tell me which way to go."

Although he was smiling, his expression was one of concentration. "Straight ahead for now."

A thrill shot through her.

He was back.

The Dustin she'd met a few days ago, the confident, somewhat cocky man with a swagger and a slight limp, had returned.

That made her happy, especially because she'd played a part in that. She worked hard to bring out the best in a student, and that wasn't easy to do when met with resistance.

Dustin completing the ice skating task, however, had her bursting with pride. The man who'd been afraid of the ice had called to her heart and made her dig down deep, so she could hold her ground and make him overcome his fear of the ice. Pushing him meant pushing herself to make him act.

Miracle Lake had been aptly name, and she would never forget the place.

Or him.

More than once, she'd almost caved and hugged him. The words "we don't have to do this" had been on the tip of her tongue.

One thing stopped her from saying that.

Dustin himself.

She'd imagined if the position had been reversed, and she

hadn't wanted to skate. Okay, he'd probably have gone caveman on her, tossed her over his shoulder, and skated across the lake. But she'd felt compelled to make sure he continued in the quest.

"Turn right on First Street," Dustin said.

She did.

"Now make a left on Front Avenue."

The scents of basil and garlic lingered in the air. "Please tell me this next photo has something to do with the pizza parlor."

"Sorry, but we're heading to the shop next door."

"What's next..." She stopped and stared at the sign up ahead. Her heart went splat at her feet. "Married in Marietta."

He nodded.

Great. Weddings ranked right up there with Valentine's Day on her least favorite list. "They really are pushing the love angle."

"The race is called the Valentine Quest." The humor in his voice was clear.

She wasn't amused. "Next year, they should call it the Marietta Quest."

"You think?"

She nodded. "Valentine's Day is overrated."

Dustin shot her an odd look. "That's what most guys think, but not as many women. In fact, no women."

She shrugged. "Now you know one."

"I'm amazed."

"Stop being such a stereotypical guy who believes women start dreaming about their wedding day when they are three."

"I always thought it was seven."

That made her laugh.

White gowns were displayed in each of the front windows. Puffy, sleek, A-line. She didn't know the names of all the styles. Nor did she want to know.

"Let's go inside," he said.

"Take a picture out here. It'll be faster."

"Yes, but that's not the spirit of the scavenger hunt or this quest."

"Says the man who didn't want to do the second task."

He held open the door. "Lesson learned thanks to an excellent teacher."

Nevada wasn't going to get out of this so she forced her feet to move. She entered the store.

The interior was pink and romantic with more gowns than she'd ever thought existed. Seeing all these dresses made her question the common sense of spending so much on a dress a woman would wear once. She shook the thoughts from her head.

Nevada had given up on getting married herself. Still, she could picture Dakota trying on wedding gowns.

One, a simple sheath, caught Nevada's eye. "That dress would look gorgeous on my sister."

"Did she and Bryce get engaged?" Dustin asked.

"No, but my family is waiting for a proposal to happen. We're taking bets if she gets a ring on Valentine's Day or not."

Dustin moved farther into the store. "How did you bet?"

"I don't think it's going to happen yet."

"Too soon?"

Nevada shrugged. "My parents eloped after dating for two weeks and will celebrate their thirty-fourth wedding anniversary next month, so *too soon* is a relative term."

"Wow." Dustin stood near the veils. "My parents grew up together and knew each other for years, but it didn't matter. They still divorced."

"Maybe that old couple at Kindred Place is right about what it takes to succeed."

He shrugged. "I don't know, nor do I care."

"I remember. Confirmed bachelor."

He nodded. "I was dating a wonderful woman named Daisy, but last year she decided she wanted the whole package. A solitaire engagement ring, a big wedding day, kids, and a house. She's engaged to someone else now, and I couldn't be happier for her."

"That's nice of you."

"No reason not to be. I couldn't give her what she wanted, so she found someone who could."

Nevada didn't hear any regret in Dustin's voice. "Where do you want the picture taken?"

"Anywhere."

"Welcome to Married in Marietta." A nicely dressed woman walked toward them. "Are you with the Valentine Quest?"

Nevada nodded. "Is there a place we're supposed to take a picture?"

"Anywhere in the shop." The woman pointed to a box covered with a heart-shaped flag. "But you need to use at least one of the props in the box."

"We didn't see that." Dustin made his way over there.

Nevada followed.

"Any exes that stick out in your past?" he asked.

"Not really," she admitted. "I've never been that serious with anyone. My parents never cared about who I dated before, but just last week, my mom wanted to know the name of the last man I'd been with."

"Seriously?"

Nevada nodded. "I told her Gus and that he spoke French to me all night in bed. I didn't mention I was reading a book by Gustave Flaubert."

Dustin burst out laughing. "Has your mom asked about Gus again?"

"Yes, and I was truthful. I told her we reached the end."

"Quick thinking on your part."

"I suppose, but I don't like resorting to these tactics. I just didn't know what else to say without getting another lecture on how I'll make time for a relationship if someone is that important to me."

He reached into the box, pulled out a white veil, and handed it to her. "Put this on."

From dating talk to wedding wear. She shook her head. "Rubbing salt into the wound?"

"Trying to pick up the pace so we don't fall behind."

Okay, she shouldn't take things so personally. She stared at the lace attached to a white beaded headband. Not too elaborate, but clearly for a bride. "What are you going to wear?"

He raised a pink bowtie. "This."

Nevada removed her hat and put on the headband. The veil flowed down her back. She glimpsed her reflection in a nearby mirror, and she barely recognized herself. She looked...pretty. And very bride-like.

A yearning grew inside her.

For something she'd never have.

Dustin hummed "Here Comes the Bride."

She grimaced. "Very funny."

He put on the bowtie. "Ready for the picture?"

"Sure." She wanted out of the veil. Best not to get carried away. This was as close to wearing a wedding gown as she would get.

He held out his camera. "Got it."

As Dustin removed his bowtie, she took off the veil.

"That wasn't too painful," he said.

"No, but I have a feeling I'll be back here with Dakota in

the not-so-distant future. She'll make a lovely bride."

"So would you."

Dustin's words shot straight to her heart. His remarks were nothing more than his being polite, but so what? She wasn't romantic, but being surrounded by the gorgeous fabrics and gowns made her feel like a fairy princess. A way she hadn't felt in nearly two decades.

Gratitude for his words made her wriggle her toes. She smiled at him. "Thanks."

"You're welcome."

A beat passed and another. She was perfectly content to stand there staring at him. Until she remembered why they were in a bridal shop.

The quest. "Where to next?"

Her words seemed to jolt Dustin, as if he'd been caught in the same trance as her.

He glanced at his phone. "Bramble Lane."

That was the street with the big, old houses on the other side of Main Street from where they were. "Let's go."

She followed him out of the shop and past the pizza parlor. The cold temperature came as a shock after being inside where it was warm.

"What do we have to do on Bramble Lane?" she asked.

"Take pictures of all the houses and then pick a favorite."

That didn't sound difficult, but she wished the task called for taking a picture of their current favorite person. That would be easy with him walking right next to her.

Chapter Nine

NEVADA WALKED AT a quick pace. She kept glancing at Dustin to see if she needed to slow down, but he was a step ahead of her. He wasn't limping as badly as before, but he was favoring his left leg as they headed north on Main Street. "Isn't Bramble Lane to our left?"

"Yes, but if we start at Bramble House and work our way south, we won't miss any of the houses."

"Good plan."

"Common sense," he said. "I'm not much of a planner."

"I am."

"I can see that. Me? I'm lucky if I have clean clothes to wear the next day. But if not, you can turn things inside out."

Ick. Nevada stopped walking. She'd been as close as she could get to him clothed these past two days, and he didn't smell dirty. "You're kidding, right?"

A mischievous grin spread across his face. "What do you think?"

Dustin continued walking.

She, however, remained where she was. He had to be joking. No person who cared about cleanliness or hygiene would do that, would they?

"Wait up," she called.

He didn't stop or slow down.

Nevada quickened her pace to catch up with him.

"You're not sure whether to believe me or not." His grin crinkled the corners of his eyes and made her take a second look. "Don't deny it."

"I could go either way, but I hope you're joking."

A beat passed. And another. "I am, but the expression on your face was and still is priceless."

"Ha-ha."

Laughter lit his eyes. "The fact you had to think about whether I was serious or not is even better. I'm going to have to call you ivory-tower princess. The name fits."

"Okay, you got me. I give up." She raised her hands. "But we are supposed to be an alliance, not acting like middle schoolers."

"Some of the best things in my life happened between the ages of twelve and fourteen."

"Bet you were one of the popular kids."

He shrugged. "I wouldn't say popular, but I had a few close friends."

"I didn't," she said. "I was younger than everyone else due to having a late birthday and skipping a grade. All I wanted was to fit in, but I didn't. I like to pretend those years disappeared into a black hole to be forgotten forever."

"I'm sorry." He put his arm around her and squeezed. Not quite a one-arm hug, but it felt good. "Just playing around and having a little fun."

When he dropped his arm to his side, a chill ran through her. She needed to regroup and get her game face back on.

"Fun?" she asked. "I thought the Valentine Quest was supposed to be serious business. No distractions."

"That's true, but I've still been having fun." He sounded surprised.

It was her turn to admit the same thing. "Me, too."

They turned left on Court Street. Bramble House was up ahead. The lovely three-story home was now a bed and breakfast. Portia, who worked at the chocolate shop with Dakota, lived in the apartment above the garage.

When they reached the house, Dustin raised his phone and took a picture. "This is my favorite one."

"You already know that?"

"I take Bar V5 guests on tours of the town all year long. Bramble Lane is one of the most popular sites with visitors."

"I've walked along this street and admired the homes, but I never chose a favorite."

"Today's the day to pick one."

This was the same street that Kindred Place was on. The houses were pretty. A few homes weren't as large as the others, but each had qualities and architectural details that made them memorable. Still Bramble House appeared to be the belle of the lane.

The next house made Nevada stop. As she stared at a neglected mansion, her chest tightened. A large pine tree blocked some of the view, but the old tree couldn't hide the state of disrepair. "Is the place abandoned?"

"No." Dustin took a picture. "That's Judge Allister Kingsley's house. The kids in town say he's the meanest man on the street. He has an attack cat."

"Yeah, right."

"I'm serious." Dustin's tone suggested he wasn't joking. "The cat lives under the porch like a troll and attacks if you go to the door."

"That poor cat." Nevada thought about the cats they'd spent time with yesterday at the rescue. "I wonder if Dakota knows about this."

"A few people have mentioned the cat to Lori Donovan, the director of Whiskers and Paw Pals. But the cat doesn't look malnourished or ill and lives on private property, so there's nothing they can do about it."

"It's still sad."

Dustin nodded. "I heard the judge wasn't always so ornery, that he used to be friendly, but tragedy struck his family, and he never recovered."

Her heart softened. Whatever had happened must have been bad to change a man so much that he allowed his home to fall apart. "How horrible."

"It is." Dustin stared at the house with a faraway look in

his eyes. "Life can change on a dime and not always for the better."

"I wonder if anything can be done."

"Many people have reached out over the years to the judge, but he's not interested."

"His heart must not have found peace after whatever happened to his family."

"Must not have." Dustin placed his hand on her shoulder. "Ready to see the others?"

Nodding, she took one last look at the judge's house. The place appeared too rundown for even a gothic setting. "Yes."

"The next homes aren't overrun by shrubs and vines."

"That's good." But she had to force herself not to glance back at the last one.

A short time later, they had walked Bramble Lane and uploaded the pics to the Valentine Quest page. All they needed to do was type in their favorites before publishing the post.

"Bramble House." Dustin typed in his favorite house. "Which is your favorite?"

"So many pretty houses." Nevada reviewed them in her mind. Two stuck out to her. The first was the one Dustin picked. She would have to go with that one. "I hate to be a copycat, but the Bramble House is my favorite."

"It's a great house."

She nodded. Her second-favorite house most likely

wouldn't be a popular choice. She'd been watching home improvement shows with Dakota, who was remodeling her house, and Nevada could easily imagine what the judge's house and grounds must have once looked like and could be again with some TLC. She hoped that happened sometime soon. For both the judge and the house's sakes.

"We're finished with that stop," Dustin said.

"What's next?"

"The park." He pointed across the street. "We're only a couple of blocks away. See the twinkling lights up ahead?"

It was still afternoon, but the sky had gotten darker so the white lights in the trees stood out.

She shook her head. "This town goes all out for Valentine's Day."

"For every holiday."

"That gives me something to look forward to between now and July."

"We're supposed to take a photo at the gazebo. No one is there. This is our chance." He grabbed her hand. "Come on."

Holding hands with Dustin didn't mean anything. He was only trying to lead her to where they needed to be. But she had to admit, this didn't feel awkward. Not after everything else they'd done.

If anything, holding hands felt natural and right.

That was more than a little weird.

Dustin climbed the short staircase, but he didn't let go of

her hand. She followed.

Maybe he was a hand holder. Something he did with city folk who visited the ranch and were under his care.

The white gazebo was decorated with miniature lights as well as red and pink heart-shaped ones. "This is a charming backdrop. No wonder the sponsors wanted a photo here."

"Wait." He feigned a shocked expression. "Are you getting into the Valentine spirit?"

He made her sound like the February-fourteenth version of the Grinch. She wasn't that bad. At least she didn't think so. "Maybe."

"Don't you mean yes?"

"Maybe."

He laughed. "What do you think? The park looks different without the obstacle course."

The gazebo was high enough off the ground to give her a wonderful view. Old-fashioned looking street lamps lit paved paths that had been cleared of snow. The cold temperatures didn't keep people from being out. Children played, couples walked, and a lone snowman seemed to be waving at her.

Nevada fought the urge to wave back. She must be more tired than she realized. "Lovely."

"In the springtime, the grass is so green." He hadn't let go of her hand. "At Easter, there's a big egg hunt, although sometimes the snow is still around. During the big rodeo weekend in September, they hold a dinner and a pancake feed here under a big tent. And during the Marietta Stroll in

December, vendor booths and a petting zoo are set-up."

"I went to the stroll two years ago. The gingerbread-house competition and the tree lighting were my favorites."

His gaze narrowed. "How many times have you been to Marietta?"

"Several. My siblings and I spent a couple of weeks here every summer when we were kids. My great aunt and uncle lived in the house Dakota owns now. My sister moved to Marietta after college to live with Aunt Alice."

"I didn't know that."

Nevada shrugged. "Not everyone knows everything in a small town."

"That's true, though many would say otherwise."

Dakota had mentioned how everyone was nosy about their neighbors. And strangers. "Ever since my dad retired, and my parents sailed off to the Caribbean, I've been splitting my school vacations between Dakota's house and York's place if I'm not off on a research trip."

He studied her. "Funny how we've never run into each other."

"Not really," she admitted. "I'm a bit of a homebody when I'm here."

"Taking books to bed?"

"Every night. I catch up on my sleep, wear sweats and big T-shirts, leave out my contacts and use glasses instead. I also park myself in front of the television and watch as much as I can since I don't have a TV set in New York."

A couple pulled two kids on a sled. Add a dog or two and that could be Dakota's future with Bryce. Nevada wouldn't mind being an aunt. Well, as long as diapers and throw up weren't involved.

"The not-so-exciting, non-cosmopolitan life of a graduate student away from school," she added.

"Nothing wrong with relaxing." Dustin let go of her hand. He reached into his pocket and then held out his phone. "Last photo for the scavenger hunt."

He leaned toward her. His nearness brought a rush of heat, and then his shoulder touched hers.

Her breath caught in her throat, and her pulse skittered.

"Say cheese," he said.

Nevada didn't say anything. She had no idea if she was smiling. She only hoped she didn't look like a deer caught in the headlights due to the way he pressed against her. Her stomach felt like an overcrowded butterfly aviary.

Uncertain, she looked at him for a clue to tell her what was going on. His face was closer than she realized, but his expression was unreadable except for the gratitude shining in his eyes.

He wanted to thank her.

For what happened at Miracle Lake.

That was fine, except...

A twinge of disappointment caught her off guard. She was a realist, so she wouldn't set herself up to feel hurt or upset. There was no reason for thinking he'd want anything to do with her beyond the quest. A guy like him wouldn't want to kiss her. Dustin pushed a hair away from her face and back into her hat. "Thanks again for today."

"You're welcome." Her voice sounded husky. He was the reason. "Happy to help."

"You did. In so many ways." The corners of his mouth lifted. "Now it's my turn."

"To do what?"

"Help you." Dustin lowered his head.

His lips touched hers. Tentatively. Gently.

She stiffened. Tried not to freak out. But panic flooded her body.

The way his lips moved made her knees wobble.

Oh, wow.

Heat replaced some of the panic. She didn't pull back.

This cowboy knew how to kiss.

But why was he kissing her?

His lips pressed harder. Teased. Coaxed. Made her lean against him.

A million and one thoughts vanished from her mind.

Hot. Oh, so hot.

The tightness melted from her body. The tension evaporated as if it had never existed. She understood the allure of the cowboy.

At least this one.

Nevada wrapped her arms around him to keep from dissolving into a puddle at his feet and arched toward him.

She'd been kissed before, but never so thoroughly, so desperately, as if he needed her kiss as much as he needed oxygen to survive.

That made her feel powerful, as if her pink jacket was a pink superhero cape. She liked the way that felt.

His kiss.

Him.

Slowly, Dustin backed away from her.

Her lips throbbed, and she could barely draw a breath into her tight chest.

His gaze locked on hers. Desire had replaced the gratitude in his gaze, and that sent a burst of feminine pride through her.

But she couldn't get carried away. She'd done that before with disastrous results.

Gain control.

Think.

She cleared her throat. "How is a kiss supposed to help me?"

He lowered his arms and stepped back. "If your mom asks who was the last man you were with or kissed, you can honestly answer Dustin Decker."

Nevada's mouth dropped opened. He kissed her because of her mom?

Put the pink cape away. This was why she should keep her distance from men.

Dustin said he wanted to help her, but his kiss had woken long-dormant parts of her. He'd made her feel attractive and desirable.

She'd hoped he felt something for her, but he'd kissed her out of pity and to say thanks.

What a letdown.

Still, he was waiting for her to say something. Only one word came to mind. "Thanks."

Though that didn't feel or sound right.

"You're welcome." He headed off the gazebo. "Let's go back to the chocolate shop and see how we're doing against the other teams."

Nevada had forgotten about the quest. Worse, the only thing her still-tingling lips wanted was more kisses.

That was a distraction she didn't need.

Or want.

She forced herself not to touch her mouth.

What was she going to do?

THIRTY MINUTES LATER, Dustin stood outside Copper Mountain Chocolates with Nevada. He couldn't believe how far they'd moved up in the standings. A glance around told him they were alone. "Are we okay to whoop it up now?"

She'd suggested they keep a low profile in front of the other competitors. After kissing her at the gazebo, he would do whatever she wanted.

Boy, his ivory-tower princess sure could kiss.

He wanted another one.

And hoped to get it soon.

"Yes!" She held up her hand.

He high-fived her. "We did it. We're in second place!"

Although he wouldn't kid himself. Without Nevada, this wouldn't have happened. She'd been the star performer today, and he owed her. Other teams had noticed, too, and congratulated her. That had made her beam.

"We should go out and celebrate," he suggested.

"I wish I could, but I need to go back to Dakota's. I have a class to teach in the morning, and I'm not prepared."

"That's okay." He was flexible. Especially if being that way meant he could spend more time with Nevada. "I need to be out with the livestock before dawn. We can make it an early night."

Nevada dragged her teeth across her lower lip.

He'd rather have his mouth there.

"I'm sorry, but I would be thinking about all I have to do," she said. "Another time?"

Dustin ignored the disappointment. He could understand someone like Nevada not wanting to procrastinate. "I'll drive you home."

"I can walk."

Okay, that was strange. He'd been driving her home each night. The temperature wasn't as cold, but still. "Sure?"

She nodded.

Dustin stood there, unsure what to do next. He wanted

to kiss her, but something in the way Nevada had her shoulders angled away told him now wasn't the time. Especially since he wanted no distractions.

Her kisses would qualify as major distractions.

He rubbed his chin. "Well, thank you. You're the reason we moved up."

"We both played a part." She smiled. "Guess I'll see you on Saturday morning."

Huh? That was so far away. Too far away. "We might need to get together to strategize."

"You think?"

No. Dustin didn't want any distractions, but he wasn't waiting five days to see her again. "Definitely."

"Text me when you're free."

He was free tonight. Except she'd said no. "I will."

"Bye." With that, she walked down Main Street, turned onto Third Street, and disappeared.

Marietta was safe, and she didn't have far to go. A part of him was still tempted to hop in his truck and follow her to make sure she got home okay.

Wanting a kiss was one thing, but worrying about her?

What was going on? And how did he make it stop?

He texted Eli.

DD: *You at Gray's?*

Eli: *Y*

DD: *On my way.*

Dustin crossed Main Street and walked another block. Grey's Saloon wasn't that busy. Music played from the jukebox, and the scent of beer hung in the air. He waved to a few regulars he knew.

This place wasn't fancy like the brewery, but the saloon was a few steps up from the Wolf's Den. He thought of Grey's as a home away from home. He only hoped he would get the two things he needed tonight—a beer and answers.

Dustin found Eli sitting in a booth with two pints on the table.

"I ordered you one," Eli said.

"You read my mind." Dustin slid into the booth. "Next round is on me."

"How did today go?"

He raised his glass. "We moved up to second place."

Eli tapped his beer against Dustin's. "Congrats."

"Thanks." But he didn't feel as happy as he thought he would. Not without Nevada here. "It was an interesting day."

"You must have done well."

"We won every task, but…"

Eli stared over the lip of his pint. "What?"

Dustin drank. "It's Nevada."

"Is she holding you back?"

"She's the reason we won today."

"And the problem with that is?"

"She's different from other women I know." That was

turning out to be a good thing, but a need to be with her burned inside him. That was bad. "I… I like her."

"Like as in friends or something more?"

"Something more. She pushed me hard today. I saw a different side to her that's a real turn-on. But I can't make a move until the quest ends."

"So wait."

"What if I don't want to?"

Eli laughed. "Way to keep things casual."

Dustin leaned back. "Nothing's going on."

"Not yet." Eli sipped his beer.

"What's that supposed to mean?"

"Figure out what's more important. The Valentine Quest or Nevada. That will tell you what to do."

"What if they're both important?" Dustin couldn't believe he said those words aloud. But if he were being honest, they were.

"Then, my friend, you're screwed."

Dustin stared into his beer. Yeah, he might just be.

THE SHORT WALK to Dakota's house did nothing to clear Nevada's head. Dustin's kiss had sent her neatly organized world into chaos. She'd wanted to go out with him tonight, but self-preservation wouldn't allow her to say yes. A celebration was one thing, but his kiss had been a thank you and a joke. That made her wary. She wanted to trust him, but could she?

She'd been the butt of a joke taken too far at Valentine's Day once. She didn't want that to happen again.

Maybe she was overanalyzing this. Maybe the way she responded to the kiss wasn't about him. Maybe she would have reacted this way to any man's kiss since she wasn't used to being kissed.

The front door was locked, so she pulled out her key. Inside, Kimba slept on a chair in the living room. The dog crates in the dining room were empty.

Dakota and the two dogs must be over at Walt's to say goodbye to Bryce and his German shepherd Rascal.

Nevada was thankful for the quiet. She wanted to be alone so she could work on lesson plans, forget about Dustin Decker, and sleep. The only question was, could she?

MONDAY MORNING, NEVADA had her answer—a resounding no. She hadn't forgot about Dustin or his kiss. To make matters worse, he'd played a starring role in her dreams.

She touched her lips.

His kiss last night hadn't meant anything. He'd been kidding around on the gazebo. Casual was his middle name. Kissing was fun for him, nothing more. He didn't do serious.

Neither do you.

She didn't do anything right now, but she wouldn't mind spending more time with Dustin. Time outside of the race.

Except she had no extra time with a class to teach and a dissertation to write.

Focus.

She needed to concentrate on her research and writing.

Romantic love as a bourgeois myth.

Just because this wasn't happening in a nineteenth-century novel didn't change anything. She knew better than to believe true love and happily ever after could happen to her.

Because of a kiss with a man she barely knew.

Maybe her mom was correct about one thing. Nevada needed to date so a kiss from a gorgeous guy wouldn't have her dreaming, fantasizing, and ready to tumble into the deep end.

Ignoring the part of herself that desired being with a man wasn't good for her. Putting herself out there, even if she got rejected, might be a good thing in the long run. Heaven knew, she wouldn't mind being kissed like that again.

And often.

When she returned to Columbia.

Not here in Marietta.

The scent of coffee drove Nevada downstairs. Dakota sat at the kitchen table with the two dogs lying at her feet.

Nevada poured herself a cup. "Good morning."

"You went to bed early."

"Busy day. I was tired."

Dakota picked up a blueberry muffin. "I hear you and Dustin are in second place."

"We worked hard to catch up after that rough start, but I didn't think you were going to work yesterday. Who told you?"

"Portia." Dakota reached down and gave both Chance and Frodo a pat. The dogs soaked up the attention. "I went over to her place after saying goodbye to Bryce."

"That must have been a late visit."

"Very." Dakota stared into her coffee cup. "Portia had dinner with her mom and twin sister, Wren. It was time for Portia to finally tell them she's six months pregnant. People had noticed she's been putting on weight. She tried to keep her stomach hidden, but she realized she couldn't hide her belly bump any longer."

"Pregnant." Nevada sat across from her sister. "She's so young."

"Yes, but Portia's determined to do right by this baby."

"What does that mean? Is she keeping it?"

"Honestly, I'm not sure."

Nevada couldn't begin to imagine what the young woman was facing. "What about the baby's father?"

"No idea." Dakota rubbed the back of her neck. "Portia refuses to talk about him."

"That's..." Nevada wasn't sure what to say.

"I know." Dakota sighed. "Portia is due in May. Sage wants to throw a baby shower, so she must think Portia's keeping the baby. But Rosie told me Portia isn't sure that would be in the baby's best interest."

"Wow. I'm glad I don't have to deal with something like that."

"No kidding. The main point of the shower is to remind Portia she's not alone. No matter what she decides. I'm sure you'll be invited."

Nevada straightened. She hadn't expected to be included in something like this. That made her feel good. "I'd like that."

"Portia has a lot of support, but you're closer in age to her than I am. Maybe after the quest, you could get to know her better."

"Sure." Nevada would like to make friends in Marietta. Even after all the vacations she'd spent here over the years, she hadn't made any.

"You and Dustin must be working well together to move all the way to second place."

Thinking about him made Nevada feel warm all over. "We're doing much better than we were, though his knee is bothering him."

"That's typical Dustin." Dakota sighed. "The night the rescue flooded, he was carrying out crates and animals. His knee started hurting then, too, but he kept on going even though his limp got worse. Strong guy."

Nevada could see him doing that. "Strong, but stubborn."

"That, too."

"I hope he knows when to stop."

"You may have to be the voice of reason."

Funny, considering he was the one who ended the kiss last night. "I'll do my best."

"I'm sorry for warning you about Dustin in front of Walt and Bryce." Dakota sounded contrite. "But you're my little sister, and I worry about you. Walt has the same concerns."

Nevada wrapped her hands around her mug. She liked that people cared about her. "Thanks, I appreciate it, but I'm okay."

"Good to hear." Dakota stared over her mug. "I came down hard on Dustin Friday night, but if you ever wanted to take a slight detour from your plans and have a fling, he would be your guy."

Nevada stared at her in disbelief. "Is that another warning? Or are you encouraging me?"

Dakota pressed her lips together. "To be honest, I'm not sure, but I wanted to put it out there. You seem to be having fun doing something different."

"I am." But Nevada knew better than to jump into anything else with Dustin. "Doing the quest has been good for me, but I'm more behind than ever. No time for detours right now. This week is about catching up, and once the Valentine Quest is finished, the dissertation and teaching will be my priorities."

"Don't let my three fur babies stop you."

"They won't." Too bad Chance and Frodo didn't nap at her feet as they did with Dakota. "After my class, I'm going to work at the library. I know you're home today, but I want to see how that works."

"Go for it," Dakota encouraged. "I'll have dinner ready at six."

"I'll be here." Dakota was the best big sister. "Thanks."

"I'm really glad you came to Montana to work on your dissertation."

"Me, too. And not just because I'm saving a ton of money on rent. It's good to spend time with you." Nevada noticed her sister's smile didn't quite reach her eyes. "I know you're missing Bryce already."

She nodded. "We had a rocky start, but these past couple of months have been magical. Christmas was incredible. I want to believe this is how it will always be."

"Then do."

"I'm trying. I just don't want to make a mistake." Dakota leaned back in her chair. "Mom keeps asking me about wedding plans and saying how May would be a good month to get married, but I've told her that was too soon."

She'd always been the one to bear their mother's criticism. Dakota had been too nice, too slow, too forgiving, too sensitive.

"Don't worry about Mom," Nevada said. "She's just happy that you and Bryce are a couple. So happy, in fact, she's been on me about dating and settling down."

"You're kidding."

"I wish I was."

Dakota's forehead creased. "But you're her golden child. The baby of the family who followed Mom's dream of getting a PhD."

"Now she'd rather I find a man."

"That's so strange."

Nevada nodded. "I wonder what kind of grief York is getting. I hope she's holding off until he leaves the air force, but who knows?"

"At least Mom isn't picking favorites."

"For once."

They both laughed.

"I just hope she stops meddling soon," Dakota said.

"Me, too." But not before Mom asked about the last man Nevada had kissed because she wanted to answer Dustin Decker.

Chapter Ten

MONDAY AFTERNOON, DUSTIN entered the Marietta library with Brooklyn Redstone, who wore a pink jacket over her pink sweater and pants. A pink thermal headband held back her dark brown hair. He carried a stack of books that needed to be returned.

"Hurry." She tugged on his arm. "I don't want to miss anything."

"We're fifteen minutes early, sweetie." Dustin placed the books in the return slot. "You won't be late. I promise."

He'd volunteered to bring Brooklyn to the story and craft activity in the children's section so her parents, Meg and Ty, could keep working at the Bar V5. This upcoming weekend had unexpectedly sold out—something rare in the offseason except for Thanksgiving and Christmas—so cabins that hadn't been used since New Year's needed to be prepared for guests.

He was down to one book. "Almost finished."

She bounced from foot to foot. "That took less than two minutes."

Dustin was sure she could tell him the exact amount of time if he asked. That was how Brooklyn's brain worked. "Now we can go to the children's section."

"Yay." She held his hand, and off they went. "I wonder what craft we'll be doing."

"I'd say something for Valentine's Day. It's next Tuesday."

"Will you be my valentine?"

"Always, sweetie." He squeezed her hand. "But you have to be mine."

Her smile reached all the way to her warm brown eyes. The color reminded him of chocolate. And that made him think of Nevada.

Would she want to be his valentine, too?

"Oh, look." Brooklyn pointed with her free hand. "Someone else has a pretty, pink coat like me."

The jacket hanging on the back of a chair was like the one that Nevada had worn yesterday. She'd mentioned the coat belonged to Dakota.

Which of the Parker sisters was at the library today? He hoped Nevada.

He knew how to find out. "Want to go see if the jacket is like yours?"

Brooklyn's mouth formed an o. "Please, Dustin, please."

"Come on, but be quiet. People are working."

She put a finger against her lips and made a *shhh* sound. "That's what our school librarian does if we're too noisy."

They walked past rows of books. As they came closer to the pink coat, he saw a loose ponytail. The hair color was too dark to be Dakota's.

This was his lucky day.

He felt like adding a skip to his steps the way Brooklyn did.

Nevada sat at a cubby full of books, a binder, and a laptop. Deep in concentration, she wrote on a yellow legal pad.

He read the title on one of the books—*Madame Bovary*. Unlike the German novel she'd had at the Java Café last week, he'd heard of this one. Might have to see if the library had a DVD version. He'd like to know more about what she studied.

She was wearing her red glasses. The smart girl looked downright sexy. He would love to sneak up to her and nuzzle against her neck. But she might not want to be disturbed and scream. That would get him in trouble. Something he wouldn't want, even if Brooklyn wasn't with him. Best if he kept his distance and didn't distract her.

"I like your pink jacket," Brooklyn said. "It's very pretty."

So much for not interrupting Nevada. All he could do was stand there and smile.

Turning in her chair, Nevada adjusted her glasses. Her surprised gaze traveled from him to Brooklyn. "Thank you. I see you're a fan of pink."

"I love pink. I'm Brooklyn," she said. "This is Dustin.

He's like an uncle except we're not related by blood, just the Bar V5."

"Nice to meet you." Nevada didn't seem upset that her work had been disturbed. If anything, she appeared pleased. "I'm Nevada."

Brooklyn's lips parted. "We both have pink jackets and geographical names."

Nevada's eyes twinkled. "I bet we have more in common than that."

Dustin imagined that was true. Had Nevada grown up being the smartest one in her class? Not all of Brooklyn's classmates understood her love of learning new stuff, but she also loved princesses, dolls, board games, and horses so she had other interests to share with friends.

"I like your glasses, even though they're red." Brooklyn's nose crinkled. "If you add white to red, you get pink. So, in a way, your glasses are a darker shade of pink."

Nevada's grin widened. "I like how you think."

He liked how considerate she was being after they'd interrupted her. This was going to make Brooklyn's day. The little girl enjoyed meeting people and had charmed many a guest at the Bar V5.

"Brooklyn is always teaching us wranglers something," he said.

"*Quid pro quo.*" Brooklyn spoke the Latin words as if they were a part of every eight-year-old's vocabulary. "You're teaching me how to ride and be a cowgirl, so it's only fair."

Nevada looked like she wanted to laugh. "I bet you enjoy reading."

"I love books. I also like math, science, and art," Brooklyn said. "We're going to do a craft in a few minutes. Do you want to come with us?"

Dustin placed his hand on Brooklyn's shoulder. "That's nice of you to ask, but Nevada might have work to do."

She nodded. "I do, but I'll peek in if I finish early. Sound good?"

"Yes." Brooklyn looked at the clock hanging on the wall. "We should go so we're not late."

"Nice seeing you." Dustin wished he could stay and talk to Nevada, but he was responsible for Brooklyn. Being late to her was almost as bad as not getting one hundred percent on a school assignment. "I have to get her to the children's section."

"I understand more than you know." A wistful gleam was in Nevada's eyes. "You were right about a certain someone being whip smart."

He nodded. "I hope I see you later."

"Me, too."

His mouth went dry. That was more than he expected to hear. "Get back to work."

"I will." Nevada shooed them away. "Go have fun."

Brooklyn wiggled with excitement. "Oh, we will. Dustin is the best at crafts. Even better than Mommy, but please don't tell her I said that."

"I won't," Nevada said.

As he walked away with Brooklyn holding his hand, Dustin glanced over his shoulder.

Nevada was watching them.

He smiled at her.

She smiled back.

His pulse went from a trot to a gallop.

Interesting. Maybe he should start hanging out with Brooklyn in libraries instead of with Eli at Grey's Saloon.

NEVADA RETURNED TO her dissertation, but her concentration was broken. All she could think about was Dustin and Brooklyn. Talking to the young girl was like stepping back in time. Nevada saw so much of herself in Brooklyn.

A chapter was waiting to be revised, but Nevada had accomplished more than she expected by working in the small cubby. She could call it a day and be satisfied with her progress, even though she was still behind. She would rather pack up her things and see what was going on in the children's section than keep working.

Yes, she had more to do, but seeing Dustin made her happy.

Nevada put everything into her backpack. She followed the signs toward the children's section. Young peals of laughter sounded.

She peered inside a wide doorway.

Dustin was reading a storybook, and the children sat enthralled. She was impressed by the way he used different voices for the characters and emphasized the dialogue with facial expressions.

A natural storyteller.

Some kids leaned forward. A couple of them stood.

Brooklyn sat in the front and smiled.

"The end." Dustin closed the book.

Applause and cheers sounded from his rapt audience that included a few moms who seemed a tad smitten with the cowboy, too.

He bowed, the motion exaggerated for his young audience.

An older woman wearing a library apron stood. "Thanks, Mr. Decker, for that wonderful tale. Now it's time for a craft. We're making Valentine's sun catchers. Walk to a spot at the big table."

The kids scrambled to their feet and ran to the table, despite the direction to walk. Dustin followed behind them.

Different boys called for his help, but he first made sure Brooklyn had what she needed. His love for the little girl was apparent in every look and touch.

Dustin seemed so carefree and a bit of a lone-wolf type that Nevada understood his lack of desire to settle down. But seeing him with the children, he was the antithesis of a hot cowboy playing the field. This was a family man, or rather, he could be one.

Something fluttered in Nevada's stomach. She leaned against the wall and made herself comfortable. She wanted to watch him.

As the minutes ticked by, Dustin helped as many kids as he could. He never sat.

Whereas some kids talked over the librarian, Dustin commanded attention. When one child dissolved into tears over a ripped sun catcher, he saved the day by helping the boy make a new one.

The man might herd cattle and cats, but he should add kids to the list. He was a natural. That made her wonder if he'd considered teaching beyond giving riding instruction.

Brooklyn noticed Nevada and waved. "Come see."

Nevada removed her backpack and set it inside the stack of cubbies on the nearest wall. She walked over to the table.

"Everybody." Brooklyn looked at each of the kids and then pointed at Nevada. "This is my friend. Her name is Nevada. She likes to wear pink, too. Show her your sun catchers."

The little girl wasn't shy like Nevada had been growing up. That would serve Brooklyn well.

As if on cue, the children on that end of the table held up their heart-shaped sun catchers made with clear contact paper, tissue paper, and markers.

"They are lovely." Nevada complimented each child. She remembered how important that had been when she was younger.

Who was she kidding?

She still liked being complimented for her work.

The librarian handed Nevada a pair of scissors and asked her to cut more tissue paper into small strips.

Dustin came up behind her. "Wish you were hanging out with Madame Bovary and Gus instead?"

His breath against her ear sent her temperature soaring. He wasn't touching her, but heat emanated from him. Every part of her body keyed in on Dustin and sent her insides haywire. She tried to remain cool and collected on the outside. "No, I'm right where I want to be."

"Good, then you can join Brooklyn and me for cookies at the bakery after this."

Dustin walked away before giving Nevada a chance to say no.

Not that she would have said that. She loved cookies. If they were anything like the pie Walt had served the other night, she was in for a treat. But his telling her what she was going to do rather than asking didn't sit well. She didn't like anyone—male or female—telling her what to do. Although hadn't she done something like that to him at Miracle Lake?

"Is something wrong?" Brooklyn asked.

Perceptive child. "No, I was just thinking."

"I do that a lot myself. Are you having cookies with us?"

"Yes." What could happen over cookies with an eight-year-old chaperone who likely had a genius level IQ? Nothing. "I can't wait."

NEVADA HAD ONLY seen the Copper Mountain Gingerbread and Dessert Factory through its front window filled with items themed to that month. Inside, however, was an even more charming little shop that smelled delicious and was filled with unique décor.

A glass case displayed cakes, pies, cupcakes, cookies, pastries, and tortes. Prices were written on a chalkboard that hung behind the counter. Nearby was a seating area full of different-sized tables—round, square, rectangular—and mismatched chairs. The odd assortment of styles was comfortable and homey. Very welcoming.

Their order of cookies had been served on vintage china. The drinks came in mason jars with lids and straws.

The extra touches added to the delicious baked goods. "I'm going to have to come back to try more things."

"You should." Brooklyn pointed to a room with glass doors. "There's the party room. I had my eighth birthday here, and it was so fun. Wasn't it, Dustin?"

"Best birthday ever." He bit into a molasses cookie.

"Aunt Rachel is the greatest." Brooklyn slid off her chair. "I'm going to say hi to her."

The little girl ran into the kitchen.

So much for their chaperone. "Who's Aunt Rachel?"

"Rachel Vaughn. She's the sister of one of the Bar V5 co-owners and the wife of the other. She also owns this bakery."

"Oh. I didn't realize that."

"Small town means an even smaller world." He raised his

glass of milk. "I'm glad I saw you at the library."

"Me, too." This seemed as good of time as any to say what had been on her mind. "You're good with kids."

Dustin shrugged. "Brooklyn is family."

"I meant all the kids," Nevada clarified. "The way you read that story and helped with the craft shows skill and experience with children."

"I do that kind of stuff at the ranch during the summer months. Need to make activities fun and interesting for the guests, no matter their age."

"You do." She raised her oatmeal raisin cookie. "Ever thought of teaching?"

"I teach riding lessons."

"I meant more." Nevada didn't want to push him as she had at the lake, but she wanted him to understand. "Like school or after-school classes."

He leaned back in his chair as if to put distance between them. "I told you I never went—"

"To college. I know, but you could go now. The semester has started at the university, but you could see if there's another school or community college that runs on the quarter system and enroll in the spring."

He shook his head. "Look, I appreciate the thought, but I'm a cowboy. A wrangler. I belong on the back of a horse, not in a classroom."

"You could do both."

He laughed.

"What's so funny?" she asked.

"I have a feeling Brooklyn is going to grow up to be a lot like you."

Nevada stared into her milk. "Poor kid."

"Lucky kid," he countered. "You're an amazing woman, Nevada Parker. And as soon as the Valentine Quest is over, you and I are going on a date."

A thrill shot through her, except he hadn't asked her out. Disappointment took over. She didn't like the way he told her what they were doing instead of giving her a choice. "What if I don't want to go on a date?"

He raised a brow. "After that kiss on the gazebo, why wouldn't you want to go out?"

Heat rushed up her neck. Guess he felt something too. Good. But… "It's nicer to be asked than to be told what to do."

He thought for a moment and then shrugged. "Works for me."

"What?"

Dustin leaned over the table and placed his hand on top of hers. His skin was rough, but warm. "After the Valentine Quest is over, would you like to go out with me?"

Tingles erupted along her skin. "Yes, I would."

"Then it's a date."

A date. Nevada's insides shimmied. A weird reaction considering going on a date was the last thing she wanted to do, but something about Dustin made her want to forget the past and live in the moment. He'd also given her a reason to look forward to Valentine's Day arriving. Something she never thought would happen.

Using the pad of his thumb, he rubbed her skin.

Heat emanated from the point of contact.

If you ever wanted to take a slight detour from your plans and have a fling, he would be your guy.

Her sister's words echoed through Nevada's brain. She had no idea what she wanted with Dustin, but maybe it was time to open herself up to something new. She only hoped going out on a date didn't blow up in her face or...end up breaking her heart.

THE DAYS PASSED slowly for Dustin. He hadn't seen Nevada since Monday afternoon. He'd been too busy at the Bar V5. She'd been working on her dissertation and teaching.

Teaching.

He couldn't believe she thought he'd be good at that. The more he thought about teaching, however, the more he liked the idea. But that wasn't possible, was it?

A part of him wanted to find out, and maybe that would get Nevada off his mind. He'd been thinking about her, not the quest.

Saturday morning, he stood in the chocolate shop with the other competitors. He held a hot chocolate, but barely tasted his favorite item on the Copper Mountain Chocolates' menu. Instead, he kept glancing at the door.

Nevada should be here any minute.

Anxious to see her, he tapped his foot against the floor. Only a few more days—four counting today—until Valentine's Day and then...

Date night!

Asking Nevada out had been a spontaneous act simply because he liked being with her. He also appreciated the attention she'd given to Brooklyn. If he hadn't wanted more kisses before, he would want them now.

Beyond that? He didn't know.

In Eli's eloquent words, Dustin was screwed.

And he had a feeling that was the case with Nevada Parker.

He glanced at the time on his phone and then at the door. Nevada wasn't late, but she usually arrived first.

Where was she?

As another minute ticked off, he typed a quick text.

DD: *Where are you?*

No reply came. Dakota didn't work at the shop on Saturdays, so he couldn't ask her.

He stared at his cell phone.

Nothing.

Concern ratcheted. He wanted to chalk up the feeling to the race and not having to do the first task alone, but he was worried. Nevada should be here.

He sent another text.

DD: *Are you coming?*

His phone buzzed. Thank goodness. He stared at his screen.

Nevada: *2 minutes away. Cat got out.*

The cat was the problem. Nevada was fine.

The knot in his chest loosened.

A minute later, the bell on the door jingled. He glanced over.

Nevada waved at him.

Warmth spread through his chest and out to the tips of his fingers and toes.

Sage rang the bell. "Are you ready for day four of the Valentine Quest?"

The participants cheered.

Nevada clapped and smiled. That pleased Dustin. She appeared ready to have fun. He was.

"This morning you'll be doing a physically challenging task, but one we hope will also be emotionally fulfilling. This activity will take several hours and be the only one you'll do. Bottled water and a boxed lunch will be provided."

Dustin had no idea what that meant, but emotionally fulfilling sounded like another service project.

"Be sure to pick up an envelope on your way out so you know where to go," Sage added. "Have a wonderful time."

Nevada was the first one out of the shop. She waved a red envelope in the air as if to tell him that he wouldn't need one.

He liked the way his alliance partner thought.

And kissed.

Dustin met her on the sidewalk. He reached out to her but then lowered his arm. No sense starting rumors when nothing was going on between them. He didn't want the small-town gossiping to bother Nevada.

"Hey." He took in her jeans, the tails of her plaid shirt hanging out the bottom of a thick sweater, and the pink jacket. "You look great."

"I had to change, and this was clean. No inside out for me."

Grinning, he motioned to his truck. "How'd you get dirty?"

"Kimba slipped outside and went into the crawl space. Dakota was on the phone with Lori asking for help, so I went after the cat."

He wasn't about to tell Nevada about the multi-legged or slithering creatures that probably lived under there. At least in the late spring and summertime. What she didn't know wouldn't hurt her.

"How did the cat escape?" he asked.

"Kimba snuck between the dogs' legs and went out with them to the backyard, but fortunately, Dakota noticed right away. I'm not sure I would have."

Nevada hopped into the truck, opened the envelope, and pulled out a piece of paper.

He sat in the driver's seat and fastened his seat belt. "What's our physically challenging task today?"

She read, "Gifts of cards, candy, and flowers are given on Valentine's Day as a celebration of love for another. Today, you'll be delivering presents to individuals in the Marietta area."

"That sounds like fun."

Nodding, she continued. "Drive to the address listed below. There you'll package presents, and then deliver the gifts to the recipients."

"That doesn't sound too challenging."

"It almost sounds too easy." Her tone was full of disbelief. She lowered the paper. "I have a feeling something's being left off."

"We'll find out when we get there."

He drove to the address provided—a nondescript warehouse on the outskirts of town.

Dustin had been this way many times, but he'd never noticed the driveway and the address sign by the side of the road. Other competitors had already arrived.

Nevada leaned forward. "What are they carrying?"

"Boxes."

"A cardboard box is the gift?"

"Let's find out."

They exited the truck and made their way to Emerson and Clifford, who stood behind a table draped with a heart-shaped flag. No mimosas this time, but they were drinking what looked to be fancy coffee drinks out of clear glass mugs.

"Greetings, questers," Clifford said while making a flourish with his arm. "You'll be given a list of items to pack into each box. Not all will be the same so pay attention. Once the contents are verified and the boxes sealed, you'll load them into your vehicle."

"Don't mind him," Emerson said. "He sees being a sponsor of the quest as being named supreme ruler of the universe."

Clifford nodded.

Emerson shook his head. "After the boxes are loaded, come back here to get the addresses where each box must be delivered. If you have questions, we're here to answer them."

Clifford tsked. "They're the minions today, not us."

"There are no minions." Emerson sighed. "Not today. Not any day."

Trying not to laugh at the men's antics, Dustin walked away from the table.

Nevada followed. "I'm trying to figure out what's the catch, but I can't see one."

"Maybe this is all about packing and delivering boxes."

He walked into the warehouse and then froze.

Boxes were piled high in rows that looked like a—

"It's a life-sized maze," Nevada said.

"An impossible one," Carly, the pixie with dimples, said. Her face was red as if she'd been exercising. "This is our third time through trying to find what we need. Dan's ready to give up."

Nevada blew out a breath. "Guess we found the catch."

An hour later, Dustin loaded their second verified box into the back of his truck. Each one of his muscles ached.

Not to mention his joints. His knee burned so badly he could barely stand without grimacing.

Knowing he couldn't continue much longer, he sat on the truck's tailgate to rest his leg. "They weren't kidding when they said this would take all day."

Nevada carried their third box and placed that into the truck next to the other two. She touched his arm. "You're hurting."

"A little." He was having a hard time pretending to be okay. "I'll be fine."

"Rest. I'll do the next one."

His mouth slanted. "Aren't you supposed to ask me if I'd like to rest?"

"When pain is involved, telling's allowed." She winked.

That made him smile. "Appreciate it."

"Be back soon." She headed into the warehouse.

Dustin rubbed his knee.

Emerson brought over a bottle of water. "It's not frozen, but it's cold. Might help."

"Thanks," Dustin said. Guess he wasn't fooling anyone.

Twenty minutes later, Nevada emerged from the warehouse. Her face was pink, and she struggled with the weight of the box in her arms.

She looked ready to topple over.

He stood and took the box from her.

"Thanks." She wiped her face with the back of a gloved hand. "The other box is verified, but I can only carry one at a time."

She was amazing. He wanted to kiss the tiredness from her eyes, but he didn't dare. Not until they were alone and on their date. "I'll get that one."

"I can handle it. I'm not sure I can carry all the rest on my own, but I'll try my best."

He had no doubt. "Resting is helping my knee. We can trade off so we both get breaks."

"Sounds like a plan." She exhaled, and the condensation from her breath hung on the air. "I don't get the contents of these gift boxes. Food, toiletries, office supplies, toys, and socks."

"They're not random." Memories from his childhood flashed through his brain. "These are items that people need, but often can't afford."

Her forehead creased.

He continued. "These aren't simply gifts. They're care packages for families in need."

"I had no idea." Her voice was low, but full of emotion. She stared at the boxes in the truck. "Gives a new meaning to this task."

He nodded. "Giving to others feels great."

But the words sounded hollow to his ears. He couldn't

forget how little he and his dad had at times. The nights he hadn't had much to eat or had no place to sleep except the old camper on the back of his dad's truck.

"You okay?" Nevada asked.

Another nod.

"I'll get the other box," she said.

As she walked away, Dustin stared at the three boxes in his truck. He knew exactly what these packages would mean to the families who received them.

A lump burned in his throat at one specific memory.

He and his dad had received a similar box once. They'd struggled for years. In plain sight. However, no one seemed to notice other than the "there's the poor kid" remarks in the hallway at school.

How had his dad managed all those years?

His father had never asked anyone for help, not even during the lowest of times, but once, a box had shown up at the door to the camper where they'd been living. A box full of food, clothes, toilet paper, cash that his dad used to fill the pickup's empty tank, and school supplies and a backpack for Dustin. His dad had cried like a baby because they'd only had a meal or two of food left.

Dustin had been so moved by the person's generosity that he'd spent months trying to track down where the care package had come from, but he'd never been able to.

Would someone feel that way today?

Most likely.

He was still grateful for the box they'd received.

One reason he'd jumped at the job at the Bar V5 was knowing room and board were included. He wouldn't be homeless or go hungry while he worked there.

That was the kind of job his dad tried to find. Sometimes, he'd succeeded. Other times, he'd failed.

That was being a human, but after leaving the rodeo circuit, Dustin knew he could take care of himself, but he didn't want the responsibility of providing for a wife and child.

What if he wasn't good enough and couldn't?

Going hungry sucked.

He never wanted to put another person, especially his own family, through that.

He couldn't.

Dustin didn't want others to see him as a loser and judge him. That was something the barn cats or rescue animals didn't do. They just wanted love and attention.

Who he was or where he came from didn't matter.

He liked that.

Dustin placed the water bottle against his knee again. He needed to do this task whether his knee cooperated or not.

Nevada carried out another box. She moved slowly. Her steps were uncertain and wobbly.

He jumped off the tailgate and met her halfway. "I've got it."

He slid the box into the truck and then looked at Nevada.

She struggled for a breath, but wasn't sitting or leaning against the truck. "I can get one more."

"No." Dustin fought the urge to reach out to her. He couldn't let himself be distracted. "It's your turn to rest."

Nevada's arms wrapped around him.

Her hug shocked him and seemed to surprise her as well, but she held on a little longer and that gave Dustin strength. Just as his ivory-tower princess had done at Miracle Lake.

She backed out of the embrace. "Thanks."

A slight nod was all he could manage with so many thoughts filling his head.

He walked to the warehouse.

Each step sent a knife jab of pain through this knee, but he ignored it. Sitting this task out wasn't an option, and he wasn't about to let Nevada down. It was his turn. Teamwork would see them through.

And gratitude.

He owed it to whoever had helped him and his dad so many years ago. The kind, generous people who'd given them hope when there didn't seem to be any left. People who, he imagined, were a lot like Nevada and Dakota Parker.

Chapter Eleven

H OURS LATER, NEVADA sat in Dustin's pickup on the way to deliver the care packages. Muscles she didn't know she possessed hurt, and her back ached. But this task gave her a feeling of purpose—a feeling she was making a real difference.

That felt amazing.

Being sore was a small price to pay for helping others. She was worried about Dustin. He'd been quiet at the warehouse and during the drive to their first stop.

He turned off a two-lane highway onto a snow-covered driveway. "This is it."

Snow drifts surrounded the small house located in the middle of nowhere. A rundown barn looked like it needed to be torn down. There were a few other sheds nearby, but no livestock that she could see.

Dustin parked and then carried the box to the porch. His limp was more pronounced.

Nevada hated seeing him in pain. She would carry the rest of the packages when they stopped.

"Are you okay?" she asked.

"I'm fine." His gruff voice suggested otherwise, but she pressed her lips together to keep from probing more.

He knocked.

An older woman wearing a jacket, hat, and gloves opened the door. "Yes?"

Emerson had told Nevada what to say, but nerves threatened to get the best of her. She had no idea what these people were going through, but she couldn't stand here all afternoon.

She cleared her dry throat. "Hi. I'm Nevada Parker, and this is Dustin Decker. We're participants in the Valentine Quest and have a gift for you."

The woman drew back. Lines creased her forehead. "A gift? Are you sure you have the right person?"

Nevada glanced at the name on the box's card. "Are you Sharla?"

"Yes."

Dustin stepped forward with the large, heavy box. "Then this is your care package from friends in Marietta."

The woman's eyes widened. "I don't know many people there."

"They know you, Sharla." His caring tone made Nevada's heart skip a beat. "Want to see what's inside?"

Nodding, Sharla motioned them into her living room. The temperature inside the house was only slightly warmer than outside.

Dustin set the box on the floor and rubbed his knee. Something Nevada had seen him do after a physical activity or when he looked in pain.

He stared at the unused fireplace. "While you ladies see what's inside the box, how about I bring in wood and get a fire going?"

Sharla's expression turned to one of relief. "Oh, please. I haven't been able to make it out to the woodshed with the snow."

"Happy to do that for you," he said with a smile. "I'll bring in extra so you don't run out right away."

Sharla covered her mouth with her hands. Her eyes gleamed. "T-t-thank you."

Dustin went outside.

"Let's see what's in the box," Nevada said.

Sharla ripped off the tape, opened the flaps, and gasped. "This is all for me?"

"Yes."

"Oh, bless you." As Sharla removed items from the box, she was quiet, but her smile kept widening. She opened an envelope full of gift cards. Tears streamed down her face. "It feels like Christmas."

"Happy Valentine's Day." Those weren't three words Nevada usually said, but she had no trouble saying them now. "Would you like help putting things away?"

"I'd rather just look at everything if that's okay."

"That's fine."

Dustin carried in wood and stacked logs next to the hearth. A few minutes later, flames danced and wood crackled in the fireplace. "The living room will warm up shortly."

Sharla's arms wrapped around her stomach as if she were hugging herself. "I'm speechless."

"But you're smiling, so that's good," Dustin said in a lighthearted tone. "Is there anything that needs fixing around here?"

"Know anything about faucets?" Hope sounded in Sharla's voice.

"A little." Dustin flashed her a charming smile—the one that made Nevada's heart dance a jig. "Let's see if that's enough."

Fifteen minutes later, the kitchen faucet no longer gushed water and worked correctly.

Sharla clapped. "Oh, thank you. I've been washing dishes and filling pots in the bathroom sink."

"You can use the kitchen sink now." Nevada wished Dustin could see that he was a man of many talents with a generous heart.

"Anything else need fixing?" Dustin asked.

"No, I'm good." Sharla stared at the box with a look of awe. "Thanks to you and my Marietta friends."

"Then we'll be going." Dustin's smile never wavered. "We have more deliveries to make."

Sharla hugged each of them. "Drive careful. The roads

can be slick."

"We will." Dustin looked around the house one last time as if taking inventory. "Take care."

"Nice to meet you, Sharla." Nevada followed Dustin out of the house. She waved before climbing into the cab.

He got into the truck and turned on the ignition.

Sharla went back inside.

The front door closed.

"Wow." As the truck pulled away, Nevada glanced back at the house. "I'm not sure if I should be happy for helping or crying for not doing more."

"Be happy. This made Sharla's day in more ways than you realize." His jaw was tense as if he'd had a hard time with the visit. "It's hard not knowing where your next meal is coming from or not being able to afford to fix something when it breaks."

"That was so nice of you to bring in firewood and fix the faucet."

"Least I could do. I remember…" Dustin pressed his lips together.

"What?"

He didn't answer. His gaze darkened.

Something told Nevada this was important. "What do you remember?"

His Adam's apple bobbed. "What it's like to not have enough food to eat or have a place to live."

She inhaled sharply. The raw emotion in his voice hurt

her heart. She touched his forearm. "You and your dad?"

He nodded.

She had no idea about his past, but this explained his reactions at the warehouse and the way he pushed himself so hard despite his knee.

"My dad's a good man and father," Dustin said finally. "Things are going well for him now, but when I was growing up, he had the worst luck when it came to jobs and bosses. No matter how hard he worked, it was never enough."

She connected the dots. "Which left the two of you with even less."

Dustin nodded. "We lived paycheck to paycheck, if there was money coming in. Sometimes, his only income was what he won at a rodeo, so he tried hard to stay healthy, but that didn't always happen. As soon as I was old enough to earn money, I did, even if it was only a few dollars from mowing lawns or shoveling snow."

"The uncertainty must have been difficult."

He kept his gaze focused on the road. "Yeah, but when it's all you know… That was another reason I never considered college. My dad couldn't afford the tuition, and I wanted to work so I could help him out. These days, there are more services to help provide food and money for electric bills. Back then, there wasn't a lot. Nobody cared. At least that's how it seemed to us. But once, we got a care package like the ones we're delivering today."

Nevada tried to imagine what growing up with so little

must have been like for Dustin. Tried and failed. "I'm sorry."

She didn't know what else to say.

"It was no one's fault. Just how life turned out for us." Dustin's voice remained steady, but she could hear the underlying hurt beneath the words. "Sometimes, things were good. Especially when we lived in a bunkhouse and board was included. But one summer, after my dad got fired and couldn't find another job, we lived in his pickup. There was a camper on the back, but that was a little sketchy. There never was enough food."

Growing up, she'd missed her dad when he was deployed and she hated moving so often, but at least she had a place to call home and food to eat. Nevada couldn't imagine what being homeless and hungry would do to a kid.

To Dustin.

Hearing about his past made her understand the underlying reason for him wanting to avoid commitment and why he preferred a carefree lifestyle. Playing the field had nothing to do with it. His childhood was so unstable with little-to-no security. He wouldn't be as comfortable with something safe and stable.

But the fact he'd broken that pattern and done something more with his life was big. She hoped he saw that.

"I hate that your childhood was so uncertain and difficult, but you survived. And made something of yourself. You became a rodeo champion and now work as a wrangler."

He half-laughed. "Sounds good, right? But to tell you the truth, it's all a sham. I'm nothing but a poor kid who got a couple of lucky breaks. Nothing else."

"That's not true."

"Yes, it is." He glanced her way. "I'm a good-time cowboy who lives for the moment. No long-term commitments for this guy. I learned that as a kid not knowing whether there'd be enough to eat from one meal to the next. Tomorrow is about as far into the future as I look."

She didn't know who he was trying to convince—her or himself. "You made a date with me for after the quest. That's beyond tomorrow."

He didn't say anything, but he shifted in his seat.

"Stop selling yourself short because it's not true." Anger spiraled at the way he talked about himself. "You're committed to the quest."

"All seven days of it." If he was trying to joke, it fell flat.

"That's just one example I'm familiar with. Brooklyn is another." Nevada wanted him to see what he thought about himself wasn't true. "You're committed to her."

"She's sweet and easy to be around."

"So are you."

"Not always."

"You can be arrogant at times with a few caveman-like tendencies, but you're also kind, caring, and skilled. None of that has anything to do with lucky breaks." It was her turn for confession time. She took a breath and exhaled slowly.

"This past week, I watched bull-riding videos of you."

He stiffened. "Why did you do that?"

"To see what you used to do. The rodeo comes to Madison Square Garden, but that's the extent of my knowledge other than one movie I saw."

Dustin didn't say anything.

She wasn't surprised. This had to sound weird to him. It did to her. "I promise I'm not a stalker or a groupie."

"I never thought you were."

That was a relief. "What I saw in those videos wasn't a cowboy pulling a sham. Yes, there is luck involved, but your ability—your talent—to ride is more important. Without that, you'd be dead."

He glanced at her. "You don't mince words."

"Should I?"

"No."

"You've done well for yourself." Nevada wanted him to see that. "Your dad must be proud of you."

Dustin didn't answer.

"I'm right," she said. "You should be proud of yourself, too."

"Are you this annoying to your students?" His tone was lighter. That was good.

"Worse."

"Poor kids." He glanced her way again. "Or maybe not. I bet you're a good teacher."

"I don't suck."

That made him laugh.

Good. She struggled to find the right words to say. "I hate that your knee is hurting again, and this task must be difficult for you both physically and emotionally."

He adjusted his gloved hands on the steering wheel.

That was when she realized that her hand was still on his arm. She didn't stop touching him.

"Making these boxes and delivering them brought back memories I'd rather forget, but this is my favorite task so far," Dustin admitted. "It feels good to be doing something, however small, for others in need. I want them to know people care. That I care."

Affection and respect for him grew. "You made Sharla feel special. Important."

"She is."

At each stop, she followed Dustin's lead in doing more for the recipient than just dropping off the box and saying goodbye. With each delivery, her heart seemed to expand. The need to help others was stronger than anything else, including doing well on the quest. She had Dustin to thank for that.

Too bad they'd decided on limiting distractions because all she wanted to do right now was kiss him.

For all he'd been through.

For all he'd overcome.

For all he was showing her today.

She was a rule follower so kissing him was out for now,

but a part of her—a large part—wished Dustin would forget the rules, take her in his arms, and kiss her.

Hard.

BACK AT COPPER Mountain Chocolates, Dustin sat at a table alone. He sipped his cup of hot chocolate to try to make himself feel better.

What had he been thinking?

He should have never told Nevada about growing up so poor. No one in Marietta knew that about him except his foreman, Ty Murphy. That had come out when Dustin was on pain medication after a surgery.

But Nevada had asked, and his words rushed out like water from Sharla's broken faucet. He'd fixed hers. If only he could do the same for himself.

Stupid.

Although some good came from his lapse. He appreciated the way Nevada tried to make him feel better and make him out to be more than he was. He did define himself by his past. Maybe he didn't have to keep doing that.

And he was touched she'd taken the time to watch his bull-riding videos. She seemed to enjoy that. He couldn't say the same after watching Madame Bovary. With all the work Nevada was putting into her dissertation, he hoped the book was better than the movie.

She walked up to the table with a pink envelope. The

corners of her mouth tipped up slightly even though she looked ready to yawn. "Our day might not be over yet."

He fought a grimace. All he wanted to do was ice his knee. Otherwise, he might not be in the best shape tomorrow. "I thought this was the only task for today."

"Me, too, but Portia handed me this." Nevada gave the envelope to him. "Your turn to open it."

Dustin lifted the flap and pulled out a fancy card. "Looks like an invitation."

Nevada leaned closer.

The vanilla scent of her hair was the best thing he'd smelled all day. Even better than the chocolate in the shop.

He took another sniff. Maybe that would give him the strength to make it through another task. He appreciated her belief in him and didn't want to let her down. Not after the way he'd been struggling through their tasks. He needed to up his game for her.

She sat across from him and picked up her hot chocolate. "Are you going to read the card?"

He refocused on the invitation. "You're cordially invited to attend tonight's Valentine's Ball. Refreshments will be served, and there will be dancing. Your presence is not required, but requested. Love will be in the air. You don't want to miss this special evening full of romance."

"No way," Nevada said without missing a beat. "I'm too tired. The only place I want to go is home."

"Me, too."

"So, we agree then? No ball."

Dustin was about to say yes, but another thought sprang into his mind. A way to view the ball from a new angle, one that would give him more time with Nevada but in a different environment. "Not so fast. The invitation presents us with a unique opportunity."

"What do you mean?"

"This is a chance for us to go out without it being an official date."

"Semantics."

"True, but going to the ball together wouldn't be considered a distraction since it's part of the quest."

She shook her head. "An optional part."

"Semantics."

"I... can't." Her lower lip trembled. She pushed back in her chair. "I need to get back to Dakota's."

Dustin was in no shape to chase after Nevada. He reached across the table and held her hand. "What's bothering you?"

She stared at the cup of hot chocolate. "It's silly. Nothing like what you've been through."

"I'd still like to know."

Nevada took a breath and then another. "Something happened when I was in college at a Valentine's Ball. I'd rather not go to another one."

"Makes sense, but if you remember, I felt the same way about ice skating."

"That was different."

"Because it was me and not you?" he asked.

"You could have died when you fell through the ice." Her mouth was tight. "What happened to me is in the past. It was… humiliating, but I wasn't injured."

But she'd still been hurt. Not physically but emotionally. That was clear from her tense muscles, stiff posture, and the way she bit her lip.

"Please, talk to me. I spilled my guts earlier." Dustin tried to keep his voice lighthearted, even though he was concerned about her. "Your turn?"

She said nothing.

Dustin sipped the hot chocolate. He would try again. "As Brooklyn would say… 'Quid pro quo.'"

Nevada shook her head and then nodded. She took a breath. And another. "It was my freshman year of college. I'd skipped a grade in school so was only seventeen…"

Her voice was so quiet he had to strain to listen. By the time she'd finished, Dustin was ready to punch someone. "I'm sorry that happened to you. That loser deserves a—"

"I'm pretty sure my brother, um, spoke to him."

He could imagine. "Good for York."

Dustin saying her brother's name made her lips curve upward. A smile was the first step.

He was about to tell her there was nothing stopping her from going to the ball until he remembered she liked to be asked, not told. "Will you go to the ball with me tonight?"

Her gaze wouldn't meet his. That wasn't a good sign.

Neither was the way she shredded the paper napkin that had come with the hot chocolate. "Maybe I haven't left all of what happened in the past."

He appreciated her honesty and had a feeling she was taking a big step admitting that. "That's okay. I was the same way. You helped me ice skate again. You've also made me relook at how I grew up and its effect. Let me help you with this."

She looked up. "How?"

Rubbing the back of his neck, he thought for a moment. He knew little about this kind of thing, but he knew what had worked for him at Miracle Lake. Thanks to Nevada. "Go to the ball tonight and create new memories, better ones, so you can put the old ones out of your mind."

"Will that work?"

The hope in her voice tugged at his heart. "I'd be up for going ice skating with you again."

A smile broke across her face. "Maybe going tonight would work then."

"So, you'll go to the Valentine's Ball with me tonight?"

She started to speak, but then stopped herself. "Your knee. Won't it be painful?"

"We'll stick to slow dancing." Dustin was about to use his most charming smile on her but didn't. He didn't want to coax her into tonight. "What do you say?"

A beat passed. And another. She pushed her shoulders

back and raised her chin. "Yes, I'll go with you to the Valentine's Ball."

"OH, NO. WHAT am I going to wear?" That evening, Nevada rummaged through her clothes. "The only nice dress I brought is black. Dustin won't like that."

Dakota sat on the bed in the guest bedroom—well, Nevada's room for the next few months. "You act like this is a date, not two teammates completing another task."

The curiosity in her sister's voice sounded like a warning bell in Nevada's brain. "Is wanting to look good a crime?"

"No, but it's strange to see you so frazzled." Dakota laughed. "I like it."

Nevada sighed. "While you're liking it, could you please help me figure out an outfit?"

Dakota jumped off the bed. "I have the perfect dress for you in my room."

"Now you tell me." Nevada followed Dakota into her bedroom.

"It's not mine, but Portia's. She thought I should wear it to my Valentine's dinner with Bryce, but the waist is tight on me. It'll fit you better." Dakota pulled a red dress from her closet. "Try this on."

Nevada hesitated. Wearing her sister's clothes was one thing, but someone else's... "The dress is beautiful, but Portia might not want me—"

"I'm texting her now."

Less than a minute later, Dakota's phone buzzed. "Portia would love for you to wear it."

"The dress probably won't fit." A pain throbbed behind Nevada's forehead. "Maybe I shouldn't go."

"You're going if I have to drag you there myself." Dakota handed the dress to her. "Try it on."

"You are bossy."

"I learned from the best."

"Mom," they said at the same time, and then they burst into laughter.

An hour later, Nevada arrived at the Graff Hotel with Dustin. Outside, competitors waved. A few said hello and congratulated them on their efforts. For the first time in well, forever, she felt a sense of belonging and that calmed her nerves about the ball. "I never thought I'd say this, but I don't feel like such an outsider."

He grinned. "You aren't one."

"Entering the quest is giving me so much more than a chance to win my brother a vacation."

"And there are still three days left."

She couldn't wait.

They entered the Graff. The hotel had been remodeled a few years ago, and she loved the mix of old world and modern décor. Fancy for a small town—a grand hotel in every sense of the word—yet the uniformed staff was welcoming, not snobby.

Dustin's hand rested at the small of her back. "Let's leave our jackets at the coat check."

She'd been wearing hers when he picked her up and couldn't wait to see what he thought of her—well, Portia's—dress.

He helped her out of her jacket. "You look... wow. Turn around."

Nevada did. The red dress fit tight in the bodice, but the short skirt flared. She wore black heels that made her legs look longer than they were. Dakota said she'd looked beautiful. Nevada felt that way. "Like it?"

"You're stunning."

"Thank you." His words gave her confidence a boost.

Dustin removed his coat. He wore a white Western shirt with pearl snaps, a fancy bolo tie, dark pants, and polished boots.

She gave him a second and third look. Forget a tux. This was the only dressy attire a man needed. "You look so handsome."

"I don't dress up often, but tonight is a special occasion."

Nevada hoped it went well.

After grabbing her hand, he led her into the ballroom. The room was crowded. Not only had quest competitors been invited to the event, but tickets had also been sold to benefit local nonprofit organizations.

She stared in awe at how magical the room seemed with white miniature lights wrapped in tulle and draped across the ceiling and along the walls. Crystal vases full of pink and red roses sat on round linen-covered tables. A giant heart made of balloons provided the perfect backdrop for selfies. The only nod to cupid was an ice sculpture.

"Very tasteful decorations." Thank goodness. "And look at all the food."

Tables of appetizers and desserts were set up around the room. Her gaze zoomed in on one of her favorites. "They have a fondue fountain."

"That's the Graff for you."

"I'm glad I...*we* are here."

That feeling wasn't due to the hotel or the chocolate. She had Dustin to thank for that.

He was still holding her hand as if that was the most natural gesture to do. It felt that way.

"Would you like to dance?" he asked.

Nevada glanced at his knee, but she didn't say anything. She needed to trust he knew what he could and couldn't do.

He led her to the dance floor where a DJ played music.

"I'll let you know if I need to sit a song or two out," he said. "But this is a ball, and the ivory-tower princess should dance."

His nickname for her brought a rush of warmth.

"Well, you, kind sir, are helping me escape that ivory tower." She curtsied. "I'd be delighted to dance."

Dustin pulled her against him. They danced to a slow, romantic ballad. He brushed his lips across her hair. "I like this. And I really like you."

Nevada thought about this man who was afraid to ice skate and had grown up poor. She'd never met anyone like Dustin Decker.

He'd shown her so many different sides—the cocky cowboy who was ready to claim his prize before the quest began, the man-child who hadn't faced his fear of ice skating, the caveman who liked to tell others what to do, and the adult who still seemed to be letting his past influence him. But underneath those layers, she saw a caring, generous man. He wasn't perfect, but no matter what words he might say, he wasn't a lone wolf with self-serving motivations. He wanted to help others...help her.

"Thank you," she said. "I'm so glad I came to the ball with you."

"Me, too."

Beautiful women in lovely dresses surrounded them, but the way Dustin looked at Nevada made her feel like she was the only female in the room. Each glance, each touch, sent tingles shooting through her.

"And since we're having such a great time," he continued. "A longer kiss might be in order."

Anticipation surged through her, but before she could say anything or make the first move—something that didn't terrify her any longer—Dustin leaned forward.

She met him halfway.

Lips touched and moved over each other.

Longing had been building inside her for days. She kissed him back with an urgency and need that surprised her.

But it didn't scare her.

With him, this felt right.

Here, now, was all that mattered.

She gave into his kiss, into him.

She arched to get closer.

Physical closeness was all she could hope for with a man who didn't want a girlfriend or anything that resembled a relationship. Today, she'd come to understand him more and his reasons for avoiding commitment.

Something so casual might not be enough for her, but it was too soon to know that. They hadn't known each other long, but he'd been honest with her about what he wanted.

But she didn't want to think about any of that right now. She wanted to enjoy this.

Him.

He showered kisses along the corners of her mouth.

She tilted her head back, and he left a trail of kisses along her jawline up to her earlobe where he nibbled and made her groan with pleasure.

His lips returned to hers. Control slipped. If they kept this up…

He pulled back.

Her heart pounded like the timpani being played during Tchaikovsky's "1812 Overture."

"Where did that come from?" he asked.

She'd kissed him with sheer abandon, but she wasn't embarrassed. "Like you said, a longer kiss was in order."

"Off to get a room?" A male competitor, who was from a nearby town, snickered. "Figured there had to be a reason you picked her. Now I know."

Dustin's nostrils flared like an angry bull. He stepped between the guy and Nevada. "Watch what you say about my partner."

The man, who Nevada thought was in third or fourth place with his partner—a fit-looking woman—held up his hands. "Just joking around, bro."

Dustin didn't back down.

"I'm ready for dessert." Nevada wanted to diffuse the tension between the two. She pulled him toward the dessert table. "Let's try the fondue."

Dustin walked away begrudgingly.

"I appreciate your chivalry, but a guy like that isn't worth getting into a fight with."

"No." He raised her hand to his mouth and kissed it. "But you are."

"Keep that up and I'm going to think this is part of your winning strategy… or you're starting to care about me."

The way she cared for him, but she didn't dare admit that.

A mischievous gleam lit his eyes and matched the smile spreading across his face. "Who says it has to be one or the other?"

No one, but Nevada would have much preferred the latter.

AT SIX O'CLOCK in the morning, Dustin's phone pinged. He bolted upright.

Nevada.

Was she okay?

He grabbed his phone and glanced at the screen. A text was there, but not from her.

> **V_Quest:** *We regret to inform you that today's tasks have been cancelled due to a winter-storm alert. Stay inside and keep warm. We hope to be back on schedule Monday afternoon.*

Dustin blinked, wiped his tired eyes, and reread the text. Cancelled.

Dylan Morgan at KCMC had said the weather would be chilly, but clear all weekend. No sign of snow, not even flurries. The weatherman was wrong. Again.

A winter-storm alert meant Dustin wouldn't be leaving the Bar V5 today. He'd need to watch out for the livestock and help with the guests since the place was sold out. He wouldn't be able to see Nevada.

Another text arrived.

> **Dad:** *Heard a bad storm is hitting. Stay safe and dry. Don't be a hero.*

Dustin laughed. He typed a reply.

DD: *No worries. Not paid enough for heroics. Got time for a quick call?*
Dad: *Always.*

Dustin called his dad, who picked up after the first ring.

"Is the weather hampering the quest?" Dad asked.

"Everything's cancelled today."

"Still in second place?"

"First after yesterday." Staying to help the gift-box recipients had earned them bonus points. Although they hadn't known that would happen. They'd just been doing a nice deed.

His dad whistled. "Congrats."

"Thanks."

"How's that partner of yours working out?" Dad asked.

"Better than I expected. She's…"

"What?"

"Nevada's not like any other woman I've met. I really like her."

"It's about time."

"What do you mean?" Dustin asked.

"You're thirty years old. I've been wondering when you'd meet a girl worth mentioning to me."

Hadn't he told his dad about Daisy? They'd dated a year, but Dustin couldn't remember. "Nevada's getting her PhD at Columbia."

"Sounds like a smart woman if she's interested in my son."

"Dad…"

"I know your mother and I weren't the best examples when it came to having a successful relationship, but don't let our mistakes ruin your chance at love."

"Like, Dad. Just like. We hardly know each other."

But as Dustin said the words, they didn't ring true. Doing the quest and being open was letting him get to know her in a deeper and faster way than usual.

His dad laughed. "If you say so."

Dustin clutched his phone. He wasn't sure what to think, but he did want his dad's opinion on something. "Nevada thinks I'd make a good teacher."

"You're one of the best riding instructors in that part of Montana. You could do more with that if you lessened your workload at the ranch."

"I'm a wrangler with a bum knee." His hand rubbed said knee. "Dakota meant more than me giving riding instructions."

"Does that interest you?"

"I don't know, but it's something I never thought about. I think I could be a good teacher."

"I have no doubt about that," his dad said without any hesitation. "There are many kinds of teaching opportunities around these days. Not all are inside a classroom. See what your options are."

"Maybe I will."

"If you decide you want to go to school, I have a little money saved up that could help with tuition."

"Dad—"

"You took good care of me when you were lighting up the leader board bull riding. Been saving some of that money just in case you needed it."

Dustin's throat tightened. He'd never expected his father to do that. "Thanks."

"Anytime, Son. Be careful with the storm."

"Will do."

His dad disconnected from the call.

Dustin dressed. Today was supposed to be his day off because of the quest, but the storm changed that. He would ride out to check on the cattle and see what else needed to be done.

And once his work was finished, he would come back here. The bunkhouse computer would be a good place to find out what his options might be. He also knew a certain ivory-tower princess who might have a few ideas for him.

That wasn't an excuse so he could call Nevada. After sharing secrets and an amazing kiss last night, he didn't need a reason to call her. Knowing that made him very happy.

Chapter Twelve

NEVADA MADE THE most of the snow day by working on her dissertation. By Monday afternoon, the snowstorm had passed, and the Valentine Quest was back on schedule. Today's task brought competitors to the Marietta hospital. Nevada sat in a large room with children who were patients there. Blank cards, stickers, crayons, and markers lay on tables surrounded by kids in chairs and some in wheelchairs.

Today's task instructed them to help the children make Valentine's cards for the other patients at the hospital. A wonderful thought, but Nevada couldn't say she was completely comfortable. She'd never spent much time around kids—healthy or sick. But based on the smiling young faces around her, this was fast turning into one of her favorite tasks.

"When I grow up, I want to be a cowboy." A young boy named Leo sat between her and Dustin. "Cowboys are cool."

Smiling, she raised her gaze to meet Dustin's. "They are cool. Hardworking and good with animals."

"And kids." Leo stared up at Dustin with hero worship in his eyes. "Cowboys like Dustin come to see us. Especially during rodeo weekend."

That might explain why Dustin was so at ease around Leo and the other children. "Really?"

Leo nodded enthusiastically. "Cowboys are the good guys."

"You're one of the good guys, too." Dustin pulled out a red bandanna from his pocket and loosely tied it around the boy's neck. "All cowboys need one of these."

"Wow. Thanks." The boy touched the bandanna as if in awe. "I can't wait to ride horses. Mommy said I have the good kind of cancer, so I'll get the chance."

Nevada's breath caught. As if cancer or any other life-threatening illness could ever be considered good, but the little boy impressed her.

"Even if it is," Leo continued. "I don't like getting medicine. Chemo for Leo is what my mommy calls it. I feel icky afterward."

"I'm sure you do, kiddo." Dustin gently touched the boy's thin shoulder. "But cowboys do what they must do to get better, so stick with it."

"I will."

"Good," Dustin said. "Because once you're feeling better, we're going to teach you to rope a calf. We'll start with you standing. Once you have that down, we'll move to a horse. How does that sound?"

The boy sucked in a breath, and then he nodded furiously.

"There's nothing like roping your first calf." Dustin leaned closer to Leo. "Your heart beats like a snare drum roll. Sweat drips down your face, but you don't care. Timing is all that matters. Because if you get that wrong..."

"You get a cowboy speeding ticket," Leo said.

"That's right. And ten seconds is hard to make up, but when you get it right... man, is it the sweetest feeling in the world."

Nevada watched, mesmerized by Dustin. She understood why Leo was, too.

Passion shone in Dustin's eyes and in each word. Love for the rodeo, too. He might be a former champion, but this was more than a job for him. It was his life. Who he was.

Or had been before his injury.

Leo rubbed his hands together. "I can't wait."

"Me, either," Dustin said. "So, listen. There's no rush. Take your time getting better. The Bar V5 will be there when you're ready. We have cattle, horses, and barn cats."

Leo looked ready to pack his bags now. "Any dogs?"

"Yep. A cattle dog named Dusty." Dustin's smile widened. "Want to hear a funny story?"

"Yes!" Leo shouted.

Nevada appreciated the boy's enthusiasm because she wanted to hear the story, too.

"When I was growing up and when I was on the rodeo

circuit, everyone called me Dusty. But this old cattle dog named Dusty had been at the Bar V5 first, so I go by my full name Dustin. That way, no one gets confused."

A puzzled expression formed on Leo's face. "Who would confuse you with a dog?"

"I told the foreman the same thing," Dustin said. "But he said no to my using Dusty."

Nevada had no idea if that was a true story, but Leo held on to each word. As Dustin had with Brooklyn at the library, he acted more like a father figure with Leo than a flirty, hot cowboy looking for a fling.

Nevada could imagine what his children might look like. Blond, with sparkling blue eyes, the kids would wear jeans, T-shirts, and cowboy boots, have smiling faces, leave sticky handprints on the walls, and track dirt everywhere. They would be, in a word, adorable.

Like him.

Picturing Dustin as a father sent her pulse sprinting. He would be the kind of dad who chased kids around the yard in games of tag, carried them on their shoulders on long walks, and taught them to help others.

The images in her mind appealed to her more than she thought they would. Especially since that was the last thing he wanted.

What was she thinking?

His kisses made seeing straight impossible. She must be suffering the aftereffects from the ball on Saturday night.

Dustin handed Leo a sheet of stickers. "Want to use any of these?"

"Maybe." Leo held up his card. "What do you think of my horse?"

At the sight of the brown horse, Nevada's heart lodged in her throat. Tears welled in her eyes. "Oh, Leo, that's lovely. You're so talented."

The boy beamed. "Thanks. I have a lot of time to practice."

Of course he did. But she knew enough to recognize a budding artist. "If you change your mind about being a cowboy, you could be an artist."

"Why not be both?" Dustin asked. "Never limit yourself."

She hadn't expected him to say that, but she agreed. "Listen to what Dustin says."

He leaned closer to Leo and placed his arm around the boy. "You know, that horse reminds me of one I rode way back when I first started on the rodeo circuit. I was a few years older than you are now."

Leo's eyes widened. "Wow."

"Wow is right. His name was Tank, and that described him perfectly. If you didn't watch him close, he'd barrel right over you." Dustin winked. "At least, he did that to me."

Leo laughed, and the sound filled Nevada's heart with warmth. Something inside her ached. It was small and unfamiliar, but there.

What was going on?

She had put her dream of having a family aside. For good reasons.

Getting her dissertation and tenure would allow her to have a permanent home and share her knowledge. Nothing would stand in the way of her plans, especially a cowboy from Montana. Yet...

Being here today—just being in Marietta–was making Nevada realize there was more to life than her dissertation and school. The interaction between Dustin and Leo touched her heart in a way she hadn't imagined.

Nevada couldn't wait for the race to be over, so they could go on their date. But she also wanted to do something else. She wanted to ask Dustin to be her valentine.

Maybe he would want to be.

And maybe, just maybe, he would want to be...

More.

Realization hit like cupid's arrow to the heart.

She was falling for Dustin.

Falling hard.

For so long, she'd kept the idea of falling in love buried so deep inside. Being with Dustin was bringing those secret longings to the surface. She still wanted the future she'd planned and dreamed about for herself, but those things no longer seemed enough.

And she knew why.

Doing the quest with Dustin had shown her something

she hadn't realized was important to her…

She wanted someone to be a part of her life.

Nevada had never felt this hum of awareness with a man, the heightened senses, and being part of something bigger than herself.

She had no baseline for a comparison of her emotions. She just wanted to be with him. And when she wasn't with him, he was on her mind and in her heart.

But were her feelings real? Could affection grow into something lasting after knowing someone for such a short time?

Nevada hoped so.

WHILE HE DROVE them back to the chocolate shop, Dustin glanced at Nevada sitting in the passenger seat. "You're quiet. Everything okay?"

She nodded. "This afternoon's task wasn't what I expected, but I enjoyed myself more than I thought I would."

He understood. Images of the children played through his mind. "Those are some great kids. Especially Leo. Sucks they are sick or injured."

"It does, but they had fun today."

"Smiles all around." Including hers.

She had the best smile. Well, everything about Nevada was great—from the way she threw her all into tasks to her sportsmanship. He couldn't wait for another kiss.

After the race ended tomorrow, they would be able to spend more time together. He'd made reservations for them to go out to a nice Valentine's dinner.

"You seemed to enjoy yourself," she said.

"I did. I've also done some volunteering with Buck's Place, a support group for kids with sick siblings, but this was different."

"You're excellent with kids. If you're not interested in teaching, counseling is another option."

He shot a glance her way. "I thought about what you said. On Sunday, I did a little research about teaching, but the bottom line is that I'm a cowboy. That's all I've ever wanted to be."

"You told Leo 'Why not be both? Never limit yourself.'"

"True." Dustin knew she wasn't going to let this drop, so he might as well answer. "But there's a reason you think I'm good around kids. Families come to the ranch each summer. Interacting with them is part of my job."

"Today wasn't a job."

"No."

She turned toward him. "I'm not asking you to make any big changes. All I'm asking is for you to think about it more. You might be able to find a way to combine teaching and being a cowboy."

He had to give her credit. She never gave up. "Yes, Professor."

She stuck her tongue out at him.

He laughed. "I hear sticking out your tongue can keep you from getting tenure."

"A good thing no one will remember I did that."

He would. "Getting tenure is important to you."

She nodded. "I'll finally be settled. No being dragged around from place to place or having to move. I hated that growing up. I can put down roots and have a home. Belong."

He could relate to those reasons given his own upbringing. "Where do you want that place to be?"

"Wherever a university wants me."

"But if that's where you plan to settle—"

"I'm not picky. I just want to fit in."

"Being stuck in the wrong place would suck."

Two lines formed above her nose. "You know, I've always been focused on finding where I belonged. A job that I could keep forever. I never thought about whether I'd like the place or not."

"Maybe you should be."

She nodded. "I may have missed a few things on my plan. Looks like we both have things to think about."

"That'll give us something to discuss over dinner tomorrow night. I made reservations."

She shot him a sideways glance. "On Valentine's Day?"

He nodded. "The quest will be over."

"You're not wasting any time."

"Should I?"

Her grin reached her eyes and let him know she was

looking forward to tomorrow night as much as he was. "No."

That was the first time he'd hoped to hear the word *no.* He winked. "Then we're all set."

AS THEY HEADED to the chocolate shop to check in after their task, Nevada saw customers standing in a long line to pay for their purchases. Portia stood at the cash register. Another salesclerk, Rosie, was reaching into the display case. The Valentine rush must be on. Poor Dakota had to work tomorrow. Bet this place would be even crazier then.

Contestants milled about the shop. Some made grand hand gestures as they spoke. Few smiled.

Maybe they'd been affected by today's task, too.

Dustin stopped her. He brushed a hair off her face. "I'm glad we spent more time at the hospital."

"Me, too."

"Time to see how we did." He opened the door.

The noise level was so loud she barely heard the bell ring.

The door closed behind him.

Silence.

The noise stopped, as did everything else.

Nevada froze.

All eyes were on her, even the customers who had nothing to do with the Valentine Quest.

What was going on? Her stomach churned from the

memory of when something like this had happened before.

Stop.

This had nothing to do with her being different. She was part of the Valentine Quest. That was what mattered. No reason to let old teenaged inadequacies and insecurities get the best of her.

"Cheater," a man's voice mumbled.

Her skin prickled. She couldn't tell who said it. "Excuse me?"

A woman snickered. "I can't believe your audacity."

Some mumbled their agreement.

Confused, Nevada looked at the faces of people she didn't know that well, but who had been friendly during the race. They'd waved, greeted her, chatted. They'd made her feel like she fit in. "What's going on?"

"Smart enough for Columbia, but no common sense."

She searched the crowd to see which man had said that, but three stood in the direction the voice had come.

"I bet she didn't even read the rules before she signed up."

A woman said that. Again, Nevada couldn't tell which of the women had spoken.

Their words felt like swipes of a sword. Anonymous ones. "I don't understand."

Dustin stepped in front of her as if to shield her.

If she hadn't known she was falling for him before, she would now. Gratitude and affection for this man surged.

"What's going on?" he asked.

She peered around him. No one spoke, but glances were being exchanged at a rapid rate.

Sage and Tim stepped forward. The look of concern on Sage's face told Nevada whatever she had to say wouldn't be good.

"A few contestants brought a rule violation to our attention today," Sage said in a contrite tone. "We hired a firm to handle the quest entries when the grand-prize value increased from five hundred to ten thousand dollars, but this somehow got missed during the registration process."

"We didn't violate any rules," Dustin said.

"You didn't." Sage's gaze traveled to Nevada. "But she did."

Nevada's heart plummeted to her feet. Splat. "What rule?"

Sage took a breath. "Family members of sponsors' employees are ineligible to participate."

Nevada's mouth gaped. "That wasn't on the entry form."

Granted, she'd filled it out quickly before she changed her mind, so maybe she missed seeing that... No, she'd read everything, including the fine print. She always read the fine print.

"I read the brochure front to back," Dustin said. "There was nothing like that on the form I filled out."

Tim cleared his throat. "Both of you must have used the original entry form to register. That one was made before the grand-prize vacation package was donated. Because of the value of the vacation package, we hired a firm to handle registrations. They revised the brochure and added new rules. Neither Sage nor I paid much attention to the changes since we were so busy with the actual quest, but somehow, not all the old brochures were replaced with new ones."

Nevada's gaze bounced from Tim to Sage. "I didn't know there was another form with different rules."

"We see that now." Sage turned her attention to the other contestants who were trying to overhear their conversation. "This is all a mistake. A misunderstanding. Nevada never saw the rule on her entry form. She used an old form with different rules."

People murmured, but no one apologized for what had been said.

Sage looked at Nevada. "We're sorry. This was an oversight on our part, but you're still ineligible to win the grand prize."

Giving York a dream vacation wasn't going to happen. Disappointment shot through Nevada, but she was okay. Although she and Dustin were tied with the most points, she assumed he would be the winner. No reason to make a scene over this.

"I understand," Nevada said. "Those rules are to stop any conflicts of interest or favoritism."

Relief washed over Sage's face. "Yes. That's why we hired a firm with no ties to Marietta."

"I'm fine finishing the quest, but not being able to win the prize," Nevada said.

Sage's gaze darkened. "I'm sorry, but you can't continue to compete."

"There's only one day remaining. I know I can't win."

"But Dustin can," Tim said. "If he has your help…"

Several of the competitors nodded. None looked unhappy about this turn of events.

Nevada couldn't believe this was happening. "We aren't planning to work together during the final task. We aren't a team sharing the vacation."

No one said anything, including Dustin.

She didn't understand why he wasn't taking her side.

"I didn't purposely break the rule," she explained. "It wasn't on the form I used. The one I got here. I assume my sister didn't know about this rule, either."

"No," Sage admitted. "Dakota is upset, naturally. She was helping out earlier due to the holiday rush, but I sent her home."

No doubt her older sister had fought for her to remain in the quest because Dakota knew what this race meant to Nevada. The Valentine Quest was enabling her to find pieces of herself that she didn't know existed.

She wanted to cross the finish line. She needed to do that.

Not for the prize, but herself.

And Dustin.

"I want to finish what I started," Nevada continued. "Isn't there a way I—"

"No," Tim interrupted. His red face and embarrassed tone brought a look of sympathy from Carly and Dan, the middle-aged couple in third place.

"We realize this isn't your fault," Sage said to Nevada. "We spoke with the firm earlier. They apologized for their oversight, but you cannot continue in the race."

"It won't hurt anyone if I do the final task and can't earn points." Nevada looked at Dustin.

His lips pressed together, and lines deepened on his forehead. He looked as upset about this as she felt.

So why was he just standing there?

She wasn't sure what she wanted him to do. Fight for her to remain in the race? Comfort her over this turn of event? Their alliance had turned into something more, so she thought he would say something. Stand up for her. Be the voice of reason.

His silence bristled. A lump of dread settled in her stomach.

"What do you think?" she asked him.

Dustin shifted his weight from one foot to the other. "Let's talk outside."

Nevada released the breath she hadn't realized she was holding. She made a beeline for the door.

Instead of going to the left, which would put her in front of the shop's large window where everyone inside could see them, she turned to her right.

Standing there, she rubbed her face. "I can't believe this."

"Me, either."

"Should we see if there's a way around what the firm said? Try to fight this?"

"This would be your fight."

Your. Not *our.*

Every muscle tensed. "I know, but I thought since we had formed an alliance…"

He held his hands up, palms facing her, as if warding her back. "You heard what Sage and Tim said. You need to drop out."

Nevada's chest constricted. She forced herself to breathe. "You want me to quit?"

"It's for the best."

No, it wasn't. Her gaze implored him. "I want to see this through to the end. It isn't about winning for me. I need to do this."

"Don't kid yourself. It's always been about winning."

"I thought…" The words died on her lips.

They'd shared kisses and secrets, but those hadn't mattered. She didn't matter to him. He only cared about the vacation to Fiji.

Keep that up and I'm going to think this is part of your winning strategy… or you're starting to care about me.

Her heart splintered in two.

He was the one person she knew in this race. The one

235

person she'd trusted. The one she'd fallen for. Yet, she'd been nothing more than a means to an end.

Just like when she'd been named the winner of Cupid's Crown.

Her heart pounded.

Oh, the situations weren't the same, but the emotions were identical. Dustin's betrayal, however, felt worse. Her jerk of a date back then hadn't known her. Not the way she'd thought Dustin did. But both men shared a common trait—their desire to win.

She'd been wrong about Dustin. Wrong about everything.

Her heart, blossoming with love only minutes ago, withered. The truth hit like the "L" train speeding past a subway station. What she'd felt hadn't been real, but that didn't mean she hadn't wanted the feelings to be.

Emotions clogged her throat.

No, she wouldn't let them get the best of her. She swallowed. Straightened. "Well, one of us was going to walk away empty handed."

"I'm sorry." He shoved his hands in his jacket pocket. "Like Sage said, this isn't your fault."

"No, but everyone is still against me."

Just like after winning Cupid's Crown. Except this time, Nevada thought she was finally fitting in. Worse, she'd truly believed there was something between her and Dustin.

Emotions spiraled and threatened to overwhelm her.

She was stuck in Marietta until July. Even though her sister was a fixture in this town, Nevada was an outsider. She didn't fit in here or anywhere. But dropping out without additional drama might lessen the impact on Dakota.

The quest had made Nevada stronger, but self-preservation wouldn't let her walk back into the chocolate shop and quit. She couldn't do that after coming so far. If that was weak, so be it.

Nevada took one breath after another to calm herself. It wasn't working. "Will you tell them I won't compete?"

"Yes. I'll do that for you. You're making the right decision."

The way the words came to him so easily was like a knife to the chest. Why couldn't he at least say something about how unfair this was? Say anything that validated her feelings?

She rubbed the back of her neck to loosen the tight muscles. "I guess that's it then."

"I'll drive you home."

"No." The word came out sharply. She didn't care. "I'll walk."

"Tomorrow, we—"

"There is no tomorrow. There is no we. Our alliance is over. No reason to pretend there was more between us than that."

They hadn't had a partnership. They'd never been a team. They would never be a couple.

Even casually.

She balled her hands as if that could get her through this. "The only thing left for us to say to each other is goodbye."

"No." Dustin reached out to her, but she backed away so he couldn't touch her. "This quest doesn't mean anything in the long run."

"Maybe not to you, but if you'd been listening, you'd know what the quest meant to me."

She'd been the means to his dream vacation, nothing more.

Her breath hitched. Tears stung her eyes.

She turned and walked away.

"Nevada," he called.

She didn't look back. She couldn't.

How could she have been so stupid to think that falling in love was even a possibility for her?

WITH A BEER bottle in one hand and the television remote in the other, Dustin sat on the couch at the bunkhouse. He'd been in this same position for the last two hours. The raw hurt in Nevada's eyes made him feel like a cow dung.

Eli walked out of the kitchen with a bowl of popcorn. "I hear you're the favorite to win the Valentine Quest. Guess I should figure out what I need to pack."

Dustin took a long swig from his beer.

Eli came closer. "You don't look like a man on the verge of winning a dream vacation."

"I'm not."

"That could only mean one thing."

"What's that?"

"Woman trouble."

Dustin nodded once. "I blew it."

"Blew what?"

"My chance with Nevada. She filled out the wrong form that didn't have the correct rules. Turns out family members of sponsor employees weren't eligible, and they kicked her out of the quest."

"That's bogus."

"She didn't know about the rule."

"Which is why she shouldn't have been kicked out."

"No one wanted her to stay in the race."

"Of course not. She's tied for first place with you, but this works to your advantage."

If you'd been listening, you'd know what the quest meant to me.

His stomach clenched. What had he done?

All his ivory-tower princess wanted was to help her brother and belong somewhere. He could have stood up for her, shown her that she did belong in the quest, and...

With him.

Only he hadn't.

A bull seemed to be standing on top of his chest. He struggled for a breath.

"Hey." Eli leaned forward. "Your face is pale. You all

right?"

"No." Dustin's chest constricted. "Nevada told me stuff no one else knew, and I still threw her under the bus like everyone else in the race."

No wonder she'd said the words she did.

He'd wanted to hurt the guy who'd humiliated her at that dance, but what Dustin had done to her had been worse. His actions—rather, his lack of them—had betrayed her trust in him. Because he'd kissed her and acted like he'd cared.

He had.

But not enough.

He'd still been focused on winning the grand prize.

"I need a do over. I need to show her I was listening and that I care about her."

"You care about her?" Eli asked.

More than Dustin thought possible. The thought of not being with her ripped his insides to shreds. He nodded.

"So tell her," Eli encouraged.

Dustin dragged his hand through his hair. "It won't be enough. I broke her trust and her heart."

That explained the look in her eyes and the way she walked away.

He groaned. "I'm such an idiot."

"Even idiots deserve second chances."

"I hurt her bad."

"On the flip side, if she's hurting, that means she has

feelings for you."

"Had. Past tense." Dustin shook his head. "She deserves better than a broken-down, commitment-phobic cowboy like me."

"Whoa now, partner," Eli said. "You've been at the Bar V5 for almost three years. Compared to the other wranglers passing through, that's a whole lot of commitment right there. If you can commit to this place, you can commit to a woman."

Dustin had never thought about it that way. "Maybe I'm not hopeless."

"Far from it, but this isn't something for you to decide. She needs to make a decision, too."

It's nicer to be asked than to be told what to do.

"I know." Dustin wanted to see what they could have together. "I just don't know what I'd do if she said no."

"She might say yes. Especially if you show up with a trip to Fiji."

"Forget Fiji. The only place I want to go to is New York City in July."

"Dude…"

"What?"

"You'd pick the craziness of New York over the sandy beaches of Fiji?" Eli blew out a breath. "There's only one explanation for this."

"What?"

"You're in love."

"Love?" Was that what this feeling inside was? If so, love was highly overrated. "So, what do I do?"

Eli rubbed his chin. "Tomorrow is Valentine's Day. You're going to have to come up with something big and romantic."

"I'd have better luck getting back on the rodeo circuit."

"You have to want to do this."

"I do." Dustin did. "But I feel like I've landed on Mars and can't breathe."

"Get used to it because if you wind up in New York, you're going to feel the same way."

If he was with Nevada, he didn't care. "You think I have a shot?"

"If she's as smart as you say, yes," Eli said. "Because a woman would have to be stupid to let a great guy like you get away."

Dustin hoped so. Anticipation surged... followed by a hefty dose of fear that he'd blown his chance. Too bad he couldn't call on Cupid for help because Dustin had no idea how he could pull this off.

No idea at all.

But he would try.

And maybe he'd stop by Kindred Place and see if Adele and Harry had any advice for him.

You have to stick together. Doing it on your own is the easy way out.

If Dustin had only listened to Adele, he wouldn't be in

this mess.

Please don't let it be too late for me to make things right with Nevada.

Chapter Thirteen

VALENTINE'S DAY ARRIVED with red, swollen eyes and an aching heart. Lying in bed, Nevada covered her head with a pillow. "I'm not moving until it's February fifteenth, and I have to teach my class."

Dakota sat on the edge of the mattress. "I'm sorry you're hurting. I wish things could be different."

"Me, too." Nevada thought back to each day of the quest. "I don't regret entering. I just wish the outcome had been different."

Especially with Dustin.

"I still think kicking you out has to be illegal given the rules weren't on the form you signed," Dakota said. "I wish we knew a cheap attorney."

Nevada appreciated her sister's support. "Thanks, but the quest will end this afternoon. Let's leave it at that."

"I just wish I could do something."

"You stood up and fought for me." Unlike Dustin. "Against your boss, even. That's huge."

"I had to try. Even if they had their minds made up."

Dakota touched Nevada's arm. "The past week and a half is the happiest I've seen you. I know you wanted to finish the quest, but what you accomplished is huge. You're not the same as when you started the race. I hope you see that."

Nevada shrugged, even though she did feel different.

Dakota stood. "But staying in bed all day isn't going to help you."

"You sound like Mom."

"Mom isn't always off with her advice." Dakota's gaze softened. "I know she'd tell you the same thing."

"I know." And Nevada did.

"Go to the Valentine's Day celebration later. Yes, the winner of the Valentine Quest will be announced, but other things are going on. You can hang out in the chocolate shop with Portia and me. I hate to think of you alone here. I won't be off until later."

"Oh, no." Nevada sat. "Don't you dare think of canceling your dinner date with Bryce."

Dakota bit her lip. "I won't if you promise to be at the chocolate shop this afternoon."

"That's extortion."

She smiled. "It's called being a big sister."

A dog barked from the backyard. That sounded like Frodo.

Dakota stood. "I'll put the dogs in their crates when I head to work so you don't have to worry about them. I doubt I'll be able to sneak home at lunchtime since its

Valentine's Day."

"I'll make sure they go outside."

"Thanks. Promise me that I'll see you later."

Nevada sighed. She had no doubt Dakota would do as she said and not go out tonight if she didn't. "I will."

"Great." Dakota walked to the door. "Call if you need anything."

"I'll be fine." A good cry sounded like a perfect way to kick off Valentine's Day. "I know how to keep myself busy. Don't forget, I have a dissertation to write."

And her mood was perfect to delve into illusions about romantic love and the tragic consequences of adulterous love affairs.

"Send me a text when you head to the chocolate shop," Dakota said.

"I know my way."

"I want to have a hot chocolate ready for you. My treat."

Dakota was the sweetest. "Okay."

"And Nevada…"

"What?"

"Everything hurts and feels dark right now, but it won't always be like this."

"I hope not."

Another bark sounded. Dakota headed out of the bedroom.

Nevada remained in bed. She hoped her sister was right because she couldn't wait to stop feeling this way.

THAT AFTERNOON, NEVADA was still in bed, but she had been working on her dissertation. Going out didn't appeal to her. She would have to figure out an excuse to tell Dakota to keep her sister from canceling her dinner plans tonight.

Her phone rang. The ring tone—the theme from X-Files—belonged to her brother York. Ignoring him wasn't an option.

She held the phone to her ear. "Hello."

"Happy Valentine's Day."

"I hate this holiday."

"Which is why, as your big brother, I must say that every February fourteenth."

"Ha-ha."

"Dakota told me what happened. I'm sorry."

Nevada clutched the phone. "I'm the one who's sorry. You've done so much for me. Been there whenever I needed you. I wanted to do the same for you and win you the vacation."

"Hey, you signing up for the Valentine Quest was the best gift you could give me."

His words hugged her heart. "Really?"

"Yes. You put yourself out there. For me. Nothing could make me prouder."

"Thanks." Tears filled her eyes. She stared up at the ceiling. "You always make me feel better. I can't wait to see you in May."

"Me, too, but am I going to have to knock some sense

into that knucklehead cowboy when I get there?"

"No. Dustin's not a knucklehead. He just wants to win, and I let myself get carried away."

"You're too good for him."

Spoken like a true big brother. "You don't know him."

"But I know my sister."

She sighed. "I love you, Bro."

"Right back at you, Sis. Now get out of bed, get dressed, and go to the chocolate shop."

"How do you know that I'm not already out of bed and dressed?"

"Because you're my sister."

She laughed. "Guess it's time to put on my big-girl panties."

"Past time." Silence filled the line. "I have to go, but I'll be up late tonight if you want to touch base again."

That was big-brother code for "call if you need me because I'll be here."

"Thanks, and I hope you have a happy Valentine's Day."

"I didn't have to buy chocolates or flowers today, so I'd call it a win."

That made Nevada laugh. She disconnected from the call, hopped in the shower, and then dressed. She made the short walk to downtown where young and old filled Main Street.

Conversations rose above the music and laughter. She hadn't thought the town could get any more decorated than it was, but she'd been wrong. More red and pink had appeared.

A midnight run by Cupid? More likely the liege of cupid-wannabes in Marietta got a second wind.

She had no idea what the last leg of the Valentine Quest consisted of, and she didn't want to know. Her destination was Copper Mountain Chocolates. She'd drink her hot chocolate, appease her sister's worry, and then go home where she would stay with Dakota's three foster animals and Bryce's Rascal while the two shared a romantic dinner at the Graff Hotel.

Nevada entered the chocolate shop. The bell rang, as usual, but no greeting welcomed her. Instead, she saw Dakota hugging Portia.

Nevada walked closer.

On the counter lay a registered lettered addressed to Portia Bishop and a bouquet of gorgeous flowers—a mix of roses and lilies.

"Hey," Nevada said.

Dakota's face brightened. "You're here."

"You made me promise." Nevada glanced at the flowers and then at Portia. "What's going on?"

The young woman wiped her eyes. Without a tray or envelopes to hide behind, her baby bump showed through the apron she wore. "I got a delivery, that's all."

"You need to talk about this to someone," Dakota counseled. "The father—"

"He doesn't know, and he *can't know*. At least, not yet." Portia picked up the letter and the flowers. "I'm going to put these in the back."

"Take your time," Dakota said.

Nevada had a feeling that was coworker code for 'relax and pull yourself together.'

"This is the first lull we've had all day," Dakota added to Portia. "As people get off work, it'll get crazy again."

Portia sighed, but then a smile seemed to tug on her lips. "It's always a little crazy here. That's what I like about this place."

She walked into the back.

Nevada shook her head. "And I thought I had trouble."

"Puts things into perspective."

"Totally."

Dakota handed her a mug of hot chocolate topped with whipped cream and chocolate shavings. "How was your day?"

"Better than I expected." Chance, Frodo, and Kimba had been well behaved and quiet, as if they knew Nevada was upset. "I got more done on my dissertation today than in the past two weeks combined."

"Sounds like a productive day."

"It has been."

Surprisingly. But that didn't ease the weight pressing against her chest. Or keep thoughts of Dustin from popping into her brain at the oddest times. Or stop tears from welling in her eyes.

What had Dakota said she needed?

Time.

Nevada didn't like that answer.

"The final task is underway near the Graff Hotel," Dakota said.

"What is it?"

"A snow-sculpture contest."

Nevada had no idea if Dustin knew how to do that. She hoped so, because she knew how badly he wanted to win. Truth was, she wanted him to win.

"Why don't you walk down there?" Dakota asked.

"I'm drinking my hot cocoa."

"After you finish."

"Why is it so important for me to be there?"

"Because I don't think you were treated fairly. I've told this to everyone who would listen, including the mayor."

"You went to the mayor?"

"Before my shift started," Dakota said. "That's what big sisters do. Walt Grayson went with me. He agrees you were wronged."

"Well, he's your future father-in-law."

Making a face, Dakota held up her left hand. "Do you see a ring on this finger?"

"Not *yet*." Nevada emphasized the last word.

"No rush."

"So you keep saying." But Nevada wondered if tonight's

special Valentine's dinner with Bryce at the Graff Hotel might end with a proposal. Despite a broken heart, she hoped so. Dakota deserved a happily ever after.

"Anyway, this is out of the mayor's jurisdiction, so he can't get involved, but Walt had mentioned a couple of things to me back in November. Both are applicable to you."

"What?" Nevada sipped her hot chocolate.

"Well, the first will be hard for you to hear, but you'll understand in time. Walt says that 'Even though we don't always know why, things happen for a reason.'"

"Yeah, I'm not there yet." Nevada lowered her mug. "What's the other one?"

"When I was trying to figure out the Home for Thanks-giving adoption drive and worried about failing, Walt told me 'Not trying would be failing. Giving this a shot, no matter the outcome, means you've won.'"

"Wise words."

"Yes, and you gave the Valentine Quest a shot. You tried. That means you won even if you won't be declared the winner today."

No doubt, Dakota and York had been talking about this.

"I won…" Nevada repeated the words. "I like the sound of that."

"You should because you did." Dakota stirred the pot on the burner. "Dustin is the last person you want to see on Valentine's Day, but you should be at the finish. Not for him or the other competitors, but for yourself."

Nevada let her sister's words sink in. Even though she'd rather be in bed with her head under the pillow and a box of tissues within arm's reach, Dakota was correct.

"You're really smart," Nevada said.

Dakota beamed. "That's because I had a little sister who read to me and helped me with my homework."

Nevada hugged her. "I love you."

"I love you, too." Dakota stepped back. "Now go."

"Wish me luck first."

"You don't need any luck. You've got this."

Even if Nevada saw Dustin? She took a breath. And another.

I have this.

Not really, but maybe if she kept saying the words, she'd feel more confident. Besides, what was the worst thing that could happen?

On second thought, she didn't want to know.

Focus.

Dustin's friends and coworkers were watching this final task of the quest. He should be concentrating, but his mind was elsewhere.

On Nevada.

Was she here in the crowd somewhere?

"Go, Dustin, Go." Eight-year-old Brooklyn led the cheers. She was decked out in pink, the perfect color for Valentine's Day. "He's my valentine."

Her young voice rose above the crowd and provided the encouragement he needed. Fitting, since he'd learned how to make just about anything using snow while playing with her outside in the wintertime.

You're going to have to come up with something big. And romantic.

Eli's words had kept Dustin awake last night. This morning, he'd met with Adele and Harry. But Dustin hadn't been able to think of what to do until this final task was announced.

What came to him was more silly than romantic, but he hadn't been able to think of anything else.

Would this be enough to show Nevada how much he cared about her and how sorry he was?

He didn't know.

But he had to try.

Dustin directed his attention and energy on the giant heart he was carving out of snow. From his peripheral vision, he saw the other competitors working, but he didn't look at what they were making.

He couldn't.

Because their snow sculptures didn't matter to him. Something bigger than a trip to Fiji was on the line today.

His heart.

He hoped Nevada would give him a chance to redeem himself.

As THE SUN was sinking toward the horizon, Nevada walked toward the Graff Hotel and the sound of applause. Uncertainty filled her, but she kept going. She might not cross a literal finish line today, but she could end her quest this way.

She zigzagged through the crowd to get closer to the stage that had been set up. The snow sculpture task appeared to be over. The competitors stood near the stage.

Nevada peered around a tall, thin man wearing a cowboy hat, but she didn't see Dustin. That didn't bring the relief she thought it would.

"Aren't those great?" a woman said to her children.

A little girl bundled up in a purple snowsuit jumped up and down. "Cupid."

"The heart is the best," said a teenaged boy whose expression suggested he'd rather be anywhere but here.

With love shining in her eyes, the mom looked at each child. "They're all wonderful. Maybe when you're older, you can be in the Valentine Quest."

The little girl clapped. "Yes."

The teen shook his head. "No way."

Their reactions brought a needed smile to Nevada's face. She moved around the family to get a better look at the snow sculptures.

A few were nothing more than snowmen or forts, but others stood out—a cupid complete with a bow and a quiver full of arrows, a diamond ring, a large Valentine's Day card, a heart-shaped box of chocolates, and a three-dimensional heart like the puzzle task only vertical.

She didn't know which one was Dustin's since all the competitors were standing on one end of the stage.

Sage stood in front of a microphone. Tim was at her side.

"Happy Valentine's Day, everyone," Sage said. "We hope you're having a great time."

The crowd cheered.

Nevada kept her gloved hands in her coat pockets. She was here. That was good enough. Dakota never said she had to participate.

Tim stepped up to the microphone. "Today is the final day of the first annual Valentine Quest sponsored by Copper Mountain Chocolates, Paradise Valley Feed Store, and Two Old Goats wine store."

Clifford and Emerson stepped forward to join Sage and Tim.

Clifford took the microphone. "We'd like to announce the winner of the snow-sculpture task. First place and sixteen points goes to Team Cupid."

That was Carly and Dan. The middle-aged couple who had dogged her and Dustin during the entire quest stepped forward to receive a heart-shaped ribbon.

Sage took center stage again. "All the points have been added, and it's time to announce who won the Valentine Quest."

She stepped aside for Tim, who opened a sealed envelope. "The winner is…"

Nevada crossed her fingers. *Dustin Decker.*

"Dustin Decker."

Yes. He'd won. That was what he'd wanted.

He walked to the sponsors with an easy grin on his face and a cowboy hat on his head.

So handsome.

He shook each of the sponsors' hands, and then he clutched a large envelope that Clifford had given him.

Dustin stepped to the microphone. "I'd like to thank the sponsors of the Valentine Quest and all my fellow competitors. This is a great way to celebrate Valentine's Day."

The crowd cheered.

He waved the envelope. "I'd also like to thank whoever donated the grand-prize vacation. That was kind and generous of you."

Seeing him so happy made breathing difficult. Nevada should get back to the chocolate shop.

"I'd like for Nevada Parker to please come on stage," Dustin announced. "Are you out there, Nevada?"

"She's right here," someone she didn't know shouted.

"Come on up," Dustin urged.

With a grimace, she wove her way to the stage and climbed the steps.

Dustin motioned her to come closer.

She didn't want to, but she wasn't about to cause a scene in front of so many of her sister's friends and customers.

"As some of you know, Nevada was my partner for all but the last of these tasks. Without her assistance, I wouldn't be standing here." His gaze remained on hers. "Let's give her a big hand."

Applause filled the air.

Heat flooded her face. No doubt her cheeks were scorching red. She was going to kill him. No jury would convict her, not after she pleaded complete and utter humiliation.

"There's something you don't know about Nevada."

"Please stop," she whispered.

"I will, but not yet."

She bit back a sigh. "At least hurry."

He nodded once.

"Nevada registered for the Valentine Quest not to win the grand prize for herself, but for her brother, York, who will be leaving the air force in a couple of months. She thought a vacation would be a perfect way for him to reenter civilian life, and I agree." Dustin handed her the large envelope. "This vacation belongs to Captain York Parker."

Gasping, she clutched the envelope to her chest. "I don't understand. You wanted the vacation."

"I thought I wanted the vacation, and I did, but for all the wrong reasons. I was focused on winning, but only for myself. Doing today's task without you made me realize I wanted to win for both of us. And I know what I want now."

She didn't understand this man. Not at all. "What?"

"You."

"I... I don't know what to say."

"Give him your heart and kiss him," someone shouted from the crowd.

"That sounds like a great idea to me," Dustin said. "But first, I want you to see something."

He pointed to the backside of the snow sculpture of the three-dimensional heart. The front was smooth, but this side had an I, a heart shape, and an outline of the state of Nevada.

I love Nevada.

Her heart melted, and her insides turned to goo. She couldn't breathe, but she forced herself to look at him.

"I'm sorry. I was an idiot," he said. "You told me what you wanted. I knew what the quest meant to you, and I failed you. I'm so sorry."

She hadn't expected any of this, but especially not an apology. "Thanks. I needed to hear that."

"I'll keep saying it if you want."

That brought a shiver of delight. "Maybe once more."

"I am sorry," he said again. "I was scared. For so long, I ran away from commitment, afraid to make the same mistakes as my parents. But having you walk away from me yesterday helped me to see what I wanted and what I want to give."

"What's that?"

"My heart to you. If you'll give me yours in return."

The crowd made a collective sigh.

She hunched as if that would allow her to hide. "Maybe we could do this in private."

"No," people shouted.

He laughed. And she did, too.

"Will you give me your heart?" he asked.

A million thoughts ran through her head. All the reasons she should hand back the envelope and walk away.

She hardly knew this man who could turn her inside out with a smile or a word. She didn't understand the feelings he brought out in her. Or why being with him made her feel so special, so good.

But she felt all those things, and she couldn't walk away. Not without giving this a try.

"Yes." Nevada straightened. "My heart is yours. I think it's been yours since that first day I met you in the chocolate shop."

He tipped his hat. "Don't you mean when I helped you up?"

"You were a faceless blob."

Dustin grinned. "But a blob with manners."

"Kiss. Kiss," the crowd chanted.

She couldn't believe this was happening. "Sounds like they're invested in the outcome."

He cupped her face. "So am I."

Nevada kissed him.

The touch of her lips against his stirred her heart and hinted at possibilities for the future. A future she'd once dreamed of happening but had buried deep when it looked impossible.

She heard applause, but she was more interested in the man kissing her back. The man who wanted to give his heart to her. The man who had her heart.

He backed away. "I love you."

The air whooshed from her lungs. Nevada needed a moment to catch her breath. Once she did, knowing what words to say came easily. "I love you, too."

Dustin brushed his lips against hers. "My turn."

She laughed. "Happy Valentine's Day."

He wrapped his arm around her. "Happy Valentine's Day to you."

As she leaned against him, a feeling of contentment settled over her. She glanced at the giant cupid made of snow. This was one arrow she was grateful she hadn't dodged.

Maybe Valentine's Day wasn't overrated after all.

Although this town was called Marietta, Nevada would always think of it fondly as Cupidville.

Dustin pulled her closer. "What are you thinking?"

"That this has been the best Valentine's Day ever."

He kissed the top of her head. "Our celebration is just getting started."

Nevada stared up at him with a heart full of love and anticipation to see what tonight—and the future—held for them. "I can't wait to see what's next."

Epilogue

FEBRUARY FOURTEENTH WAS the start of something special with Nevada—something lasting. Dustin didn't want the day to end. He parked in front of Dakota's house. Only the porch light was on.

He hopped out of his truck and walked around to the passenger side. The temperature was below freezing, but he hadn't felt cold all evening. Not on stage earlier or after eating at the Main Street Diner.

Was that what love felt like? All over warmth?

As he opened the door for Nevada, her smile brought both relief and gratitude that he'd been given a second chance. She was everything he hadn't known he needed. He wasn't about to screw this up.

"Thanks." She slid out of the truck. "Would you like to come inside?"

"Yes, but you have a class to teach tomorrow."

"It's not that late."

That was good enough for him. He reached behind her seat and grabbed a heart-covered gift bag.

"What's that?" she asked.

"No peeking. You'll see soon enough."

Her face dropped. "I bought you a card, but I didn't get you a present."

"You're here with me. That's the best gift of all."

She rewarded him with a kiss.

Inside, they removed their jackets and gloves. Nevada let the dogs out of their crates and asked Dustin to wait as she ran upstairs.

He lit a fire and then sat on the couch.

Logs crackled in the fireplace. Two small dogs laid on a large pillow and gnawed on bones. A white cat slept on a chair.

There was no place he'd rather be.

A few minutes later, Nevada sat next to Dustin and handed him a red envelope. "This is for you."

He opened it and read the card. The words and sentiment touched his heart. He hadn't thought he could ever be this happy. "I will be your valentine. Today, tomorrow, and fifty years from now."

She nodded. "We can be just like Adele and Harry."

"Yes." Dustin wasn't about to tell Nevada that the couple from Kindred Place had eight children, but one of these days, he would. He handed her the gift bag. "Happy Valentine's Day."

As Nevada removed sheets of tissue paper, anticipation had him inching closer to her.

"It's a book." She pulled it out. "*Pride and Prejudice.*"

He thought she'd like a book better than chocolates or flowers. "You've probably read this one, but Lesley said it's a classic romance. A keeper. I thought what better way to start thinking in terms of happily ever after than by reading romantic literature to each other."

Her lips parted. "You want to read this aloud?"

He nodded.

"And happily ever after?" she asked.

"Nothing less will do."

Nevada's eyes gleamed. "I used to hate Valentine's Day, but thanks to you, it's my new favorite holiday."

"Mine, too."

She threw her arms around him. "I love you, Dustin Decker."

As he hugged her, his whole body felt like it was smiling, including his knee. "I love you, Nevada Parker."

She kissed him—a kiss full of longing and dreams. Not just hers, but his, too.

An unfamiliar sense of contentment settled over him. He knew it was due to Nevada.

Dustin had nothing to prove to anyone, including himself. The Valentine Quest had helped find his heart and his future. That was the true grand prize—one he and Nevada could share.

Forever.

The End

You'll love the next book in…

Love at the Chocolate Shop series

Available now at your favorite online retailer!

About the Author

USA Today Bestselling author **Melissa McClone** has
published over twenty-five novels with Harlequin and been
nominated for Romance Writers of America's RITA award.
She lives in the Pacific Northwest with her husband, three
school-aged children, two spoiled Norwegian Elkhounds and
cats who think they rule the house. For more on Melissa's
books, visit her website: www.melissamcclone.com

Thank you for reading

The Valentine Quest

If you enjoyed this book, you can find more from all our great authors at TulePublishing.com, or from your favorite online retailer.

TULE
PUBLISHING

Made in the USA
Columbia, SC
23 January 2018